Bl

D0194783

IN THE WAKE

IN THE WAKE

Per Petterson

Translated from the Norwegian
by Anne Born

Thomas Dunne Books / St. Martin's Press
New York

THOMAS DUNNE BOOKS.
An imprint of St. Martin's Press.

www.stmartins.com

ISBN-13: 978-0-312-34383-5
ISBN-10: 0-312-34383-3

First published in Norway under the title *I Kjølvannet* by Forlaget Oktober A/S

First U.S. Edition: August 2006

10 9 8 7 6 5 4 3 2 1

IN THE WAKE

It was something to do with a face. I had never seen it before, yet I did recognise it, but as it comes to me now, the thought of it is unpleasant. Someone gave me a gin. I had had enough already. I see my hand around the glass, the glass is full to the brim, and then I do not remember anything more except that face, and now I stand with my forehead against the glass of this bookshop door, and I kick at the door. They have to let me in. I do not know how long I have been standing here. I have been out of this world and now I am back, and I don't feel well. Why doesn't someone come and let me in? I kick the door. People are passing on the pavement behind me, but I don't turn round, just squeeze my face to the glass and my nose is flattened and I stare at the rows of books. It is dark in there, but light outside. It is morning, the sun feels hot on my neck, but I dare not turn round. That glass of gin was yesterday and miles and miles from this street in central Oslo.

Someone gives a little cough and says: "I don't think there's anyone there yet. It's probably too early."

I know that voice, it's the lady from the kiosk next

door. I have known it for years. She is right behind me. I could pick her out with my eyes shut in the middle of Aker Brugge on a crowded Saturday afternoon in June. I've been buying Petterøe 3 tobacco and *Dagbladet* and a Kvikk Lunsj chocolate bar from her since 1981. And then I remember. I do not work here any more. I haven't worked here for three years. I stand perfectly still holding my breath and wait for her to go away. It is a good idea not to breathe, my side hurts every time I suck the air in. But then I have to breathe, and there is a squeak from my throat or further down, and the pain in my side is there at once. It is lung cancer, I'm convinced it is, and I feel so sad because I have lung cancer and will certainly not be here for long.

It is quiet behind me now so she must have gone, and then I start to cry, with my nose pressed to the glass door, and I look in at the rows of books, see that the shop has grown since I stopped working there, more floor space with more shelves for many more books I shall never read because I am going to die of lung cancer.

I am forty-three. When my father was this age I had just been born, and he never touched a cigarette in his whole life. He only had a drink with Sunday dinner; one pint because he deserved it. The body should be a temple of life, he said, not a whited sepulchre. He was a skier and a boxer, and when he breathed, the air went straight into his lungs, and did no harm at all for the air was much cleaner then. If he ever coughed, it was because he had a cold, and he rarely did. Now he is dead, but through no fault of his own. If I die now it will definitely be my fault. That is the difference between us, and it is a big difference.

I cough and look down; I see my hands. They have an emptiness I cannot account for and they are dirty, there are grazes on both palms, but I feel no pain. They just hang there. Then I remember a high grey wall and its rough surface, I am falling and holding on at the same time, and I remember utterly still water in a pool, chlorine blue water with black lines on the bottom. It is a public swimming pool, and it is not yet open, it is quite silent, only a man all in white walking by the side of the pool, and I try to work out just where it is that I am standing watching this from, but I can't. I am all over the place, I am like God, I am omnipresent. I can see the clock on the wall quite clearly, but I cannot make out what the time is. There is a palm tree in one corner. It is Bislett baths, I think. Then the grey wall is Bislett stadium. But I have not been to Bislett stadium since I was ten and with my father and saw Raufoss beat Vålerenga FC two-nil. He was shattered. Didn't say a word all the way home.

I feel the sun on my neck, it is burning or *something* is burning, and maybe it is Sunday. I don't remember. I see only my eyes in the glass and the books beyond, and I don't know what day it is.

3

"Go and see what the weather is like," my brother would say every time it was Sunday morning and winter, and I would have to get out of the bottom bunk and go to the window and pull the heavy curtain aside and look out through the frost flowers.

"It's sunny," I say, "sunshine and fine weather."

"Sunshine," he says, "fucking shit."

"Fucking shit," I say, and the snow was so white it hurt your eyes, and the smell of frying bacon floated up from downstairs, and we knew that *he* had been awake for several hours, preparing the skis and loading the rucksacks. Now they were ready in the hall with the thermos and sandwiches in the side pockets and extra sweaters and socks and ski scrapers and three lots of Swix varnish in case of a sudden thaw or if the mercury dropped, and two oranges apiece and perhaps a Kvikk Lunsj chocolate bar if we were lucky, and the rucksack would be sure to weigh twenty kilos each.

But that is a lifetime ago, and he has been dead for nearly six years. I remember an office on Drammensvei with a red cross on the door, a fireman is showing a video from the inside of the boat with a landscape of half-naked, prone bodies: THE CORRIDOR OF DEATH, the front page of *Verdens Gang* said, that video was on the inside of my eyes; skin, I see skin, velvety dull in the flickering light of a lamp moving onwards, restless shadows between elbows and hips, shoulder blades and necks, a sea of hushed softness where nothing moves but the light which brings life to what is not living. The camera runs and pauses for a moment before what has turned black, where the flames have devoured it all, finished the job, and then it swings into a cabin where a woolly penguin lies alone on a bunk, the door to the bathroom ajar, the dark crack hiding the bath's obvious secret. My feet are freezing as I stand here with my nose to the door remembering the cold creeping into my feet that time in that office, and my stomach wildly burning. But my face was calm, and the woman sitting next to me said:

"Rewind, for heaven's sake, I have to see that penguin one more time." An air-raid shelter in Baghdad was what I thought, for a year had passed, I do not know where, and it was spring 1991 with surgical bombing, electronic warfare, a war on the screen, a video game.

"Rewind," she said again and again, and the fireman *did*, goddamnit, and she turned to stone.

I really don't feel well. The cold crawls from my feet to my hips and I start to tremble, my teeth chatter, my forehead shudders against the glass as it does when you sit on a bus with your head against the window, gazing out, and the diesel engine makes everything vibrate. I think I am going to be sick, but I mustn't be sick here. People go by on the pavement, and it can't be Sunday because I hear from their voices that they are young, students from the business school next door, and as they pass me they stop talking, and I will not turn and look at them looking at me. I look down at my shoes. They are scuffed, my shirt is hanging out of my trousers below the unzipped jacket, and I see my belt dangling in front of my half-open flies. They were not like that yesterday. When did those trousers come undone? Perhaps I have been raped. Perhaps someone dragged me into a doorway on my way past Bislett stadium or into a changing room at Bislett baths and grossly abused my butt while I was out of this world. I close my eyes and concentrate, hunting for traces all through my body; some remnant soreness, and what I do discover is that I feel wretched. It isn't easy to say what is what. I have to see a doctor. I may test positive. There are people in this town who would not blink twice at planting a seed in my blood, a virus that will tick and go deep inside what is me and one day after several years, when I least expect it, explode like a time bomb, one day when my life does not look as it does right now, a day when I have the sun on my face.

I take a deep breath. The pain in my side damn near makes me jump. It's my lungs, I had forgotten. I groan. Someone behind me stops and says something I do not want to hear. I stand very still, waiting, and then I hum a bit, and the someone walks off again. I raise my right hand to feel whether my hair is wet. It is bone dry and feels as stiff as a doormat and far from clean. I could do with a shower, a shower and a steam bath. I like steam baths these days. I did not before. I always dreaded the walk from the bus stop to Torggata baths and then up the stone steps to the cloakroom and the showers, and it was cold in the changing room and in the shower room before the water was turned on, but when the warm water ran through my hair and down my neck, over shoulders and stomach, it felt good, and I closed my eyes and wanted to go on standing there. It was fine, for a moment everything was just fine.

"Open your eyes and come along," he said and opened the door to the steam bath and I went in, because nobody had told me that you could say no. I went in and there was a blazing creature with a power that sucked each breath from my throat much faster than I could keep up with, and very soon I was empty, and fighting for air.

"It's important to sweat all the shit out," he said, "turn your insides out and really cleanse yourself," but I could not sweat. I stood in the steam, dry and thin, and saw the naked men along the benches, heads in hands, glistening, panting, with their big stomachs on their thighs and their big cocks, and none of them could speak because the creature had swallowed the air and pushed against the walls, and there was no space left for anything else. And I could not sweat. I was eight years old, my skin burned, and I did not know it was important to be cleansed, that the inside of my body was not clean, where my thoughts lived, and the soul.

I walked unsteadily across the floor to the trickle of water running from a tap on the wall and into a porcelain sink, and I drank and drank, and when I had finished he came over, filled his hands with water and let it run over the stones so the stove spat loudly and fresh steam poured forth, and the men on the benches grumbled. He laughed and bent down, put his hands flat on the floor and swung himself up into a hand-stand, stretched his legs up together and with his heels lightly touching the burning wall he smiled upside down and started to do push-ups with his head tapping the floor and his legs straight up. His cock bounced against his flat stomach with a sound I could have done without, his muscles swelled under his shiny skin, and sweat poured down his chest. He could breathe where no-one else could, and I counted to myself half aloud: ten, eleven, twelve and on as I always did when he did that kind of thing. I kept my eyes on his body, up and down, up and down, and knew I would never look like that if I lived to be a hundred, not *that* graceful, not *that* solid, and I remember the hospital chapel where we had to fetch the coffins many years later. They were ranged in a line along the wall, and outside, the long black cars waited in line on the drive. We could see them through the windows, the cars stood quite still with their back doors open, and one driver had his back turned and his elbow against the bonnet, smoking and looking down at Holberggate, and the man from the undertakers cleared his throat and said: "First, I ought perhaps to say that the coffins probably are not as heavy as might be expected." He ran a hand through his hair, looking desperate, and we glanced at each other, my brother and I, and then we bent down, took hold of the handles and lifted, and we just stared straight ahead when we realised he was right.

I am so tired. I lean my whole weight against the door. I could fall asleep now, and maybe I *am* asleep, and dreaming, or maybe remembering a dream. I am in the apartment at Veitvet. My mother and father are there, and my two younger brothers. I know they are dead, and I know that they know, but we do not talk about it. I try to figure out how they could have come back. Suddenly I cannot remember where their graves are, but it can't be far away, maybe on the lawn by the hedge beside the road. The apartment looks as it did then, in May of that year; half-empty bookshelves, a pile of pictures on the coffee table, cardboard boxes on the floor. The clock on the wall has stopped. They go around helping me, giving me things they think I should have, and I find books I imagine my daughters would like. I take a few small things for myself and sneak them away, put them in the pocket of my jacket, and then I feel bad because I am cheating my brother, so I take them out again. All the while I can hear them talking softly in the living room. I go up to the next floor and into the room that once was mine. I open the

9

window and put my head out. On the balcony below me, my father is standing in the sun. He stands quite calmly, his eyes closed and arms crossed. He fills his shirt completely. It is quiet, he is fine, but I don't like the neighbours to see a dead man standing on the balcony sunning himself. I close the window and go down again. At the bottom of the stairs is the old wooden bookcase with carvings along the top and the sides. I sit on the floor and lean my head against the middle shelf as I have done so many times before. I press against the books and then everything broadens out and I can look in. There are rows of books in many layers, it is a whole room with yellow light streaming in from a window I have never seen before, and it fills me with wonder, and yet everything is familiar. I take hold of Tolstoy with one hand and Nansen with the other and pull myself right in. It closes behind me and the whole time I hear them talking softly in the living room.

I straighten up, my face lets go of the door and I stand without a foothold in the world, listening. I hear no steps from either side and then I undo my jeans and push my shirt down as well as I can as fast as I can, and try to do up my flies. It's not easy, my empty hands are stiff and have hardly any feeling, and the buttons are obstinate. One of them gets into the wrong buttonhole, but I get it done eventually. I try to do my jacket up, but the zip is ruined, it's hanging loose, several teeth are missing at the bottom so I can't fit the ends together. Maybe someone has tried to tear it off. I think about the dream and remember I had it several years ago, that I wrote it down, that I put it away somewhere. So I have not been asleep. I look around me on both sides. It is all quiet on the street. I take a few steps along the big display window, the glass glitters, it is spring sweeping in from the fjord and brushing my neck as it passes, and the latest books are behind the glass. Rick Bass has brought out another collection. I have been waiting for it. I like his stories, they are full of landscape and air and you can smell the pine needles and the heather a long way off.

I must get out of this town. I clench my fists and then I get it. My briefcase has gone. I turn and look back, but there's only a bundle of newspapers by the door. I look all the way down the street, past the business school to the city workers' offices on the corner, but there's nothing there, not a shadow, nothing but fag ends students have dropped on the pavement and an "open" sign outside the little sixties café.

It was only an old leather briefcase of the kind working people used a long time ago, they had them on their laps in the bus on the way to work, and in them the *Arbeiderbladet* and sandwich box and betting slip. We found three of them left in the bedroom cupboard when we cleared out the apartment. None of them had been used, so he must have been thinking ahead to the days of his pension and bought them cheap out of surplus stock, and they had lasted longer than he had expected. He had written his name in marking ink on the inside of the flap in letters he learned at school some time in the twenties, and as my brother used a yuppie briefcase I took all three. I use them constantly, there have been shots of me in the paper carrying one of those cases, and when people come up behind me calling and I turn round, they say: "Hi, Arvid, I recognised you by the briefcase."

There was a fat notebook in that case almost filled with writing, and my glasses which cost 2000 kroner and a book by Alice Munro, *Friend of My Youth*. I am reading it for the third time, I have all her books, because there is a substance there, and a coherence that does not embellish, but conveys that nothing is in vain no matter what we have done, if we only look back, before its's too late.

I don't know. I don't know if that is true. I am a bit dizzy because I dare not breathe deeply, it hurts so much every time I try that I hold back, and then there is not enough oxygen for the brain. I wipe my hands on my trousers, clear my throat and walk into the kiosk. There is room for three inside if you keep your elbows tucked in. She is squeezed between the counter and the shelves of cigarettes. I take the *Dagblad* from the stand and say: "*Dagbla'* and a Coke."

She says nothing and her eyes grow round with

surprise behind her glasses, and they do not look at me but at something just by my ear. I raise my hand, but there is only my ear. I try again and she gives a little cough again and a cautious smile, standing very still. She does not understand what I say. The sound of the words is perfectly clear in my head, but they are not the ones that she is hearing. I don't know what she hears. Then I see the fridge full of bottles on the outside of the counter. Of course, it is self-service. I turn and take hold of the handle, and because I feel so weak I pull it rather hard so I will not be embarrassed if it wont open at the first try. The door flies open, the fridge shakes and two bottles come sailing out, crash to the floor and roll away, but they do not break, they are half-litre plastic ones. One is a Fanta, the other a Coke. I bend down and wince as the pain in my side stabs at me, and I pick them up like a very old man and put the Fanta back in the fridge and the Coke on the counter. She doesn't say a word, just looks straight past me with her round eyes. I feel in my jacket pocket and mercifully find my wallet there. It is a miracle, I realise that. I open it cautiously. The Visa card is in its place and the bonus cards for Shell and Fina and Texaco and the library cards for Lørenskog and Rælingen. But no sign of notes and coins. She looks at my wallet and I take out the Visa card instead and then she stares at it as if it were a completely new invention. I look at the till. It might date from the early sixties, and anyway it does not have a card facility. I don't know what to do. I am so thirsty I can think of nothing else. She clears her throat and says distinctly and very slowly with generous movements of her mouth so I can read her lips: "You need not pay. It's on the house." She looks straight at me for the first time and gives me a big smile. It is an offer I cannot refuse. I ought to say something. I lick my lips, but my mouth is totally dry, my tongue swollen, and then I just pick up the Visa card and the newspaper and the Coke and back out of the kiosk. The light is blinding, so I walk diagonally across the street to avoid the sun and over the car park where there used to be a Texaco station and between the museums towards the University Hall and the railway station. Halfway there I can hold out no longer. I stop and open the bottle. The brown Coke spurts out of the nozzle all over my trousers, my shoes and the newspaper. I start to weep. I have been on my way down for a long time, and now I am there. At rock bottom. I hold the bottle away from my body until it stops running and then, weeping, drink what little is left, and I throw the empty bottle into the nearest litter bin. I chuck the wet paper after it. Without glasses I couldn't read it anyway. And then I walk on.

2

There is a ringing sound. I wake and I switch the alarm clock off. It goes on ringing. I fumble for the telephone in the dark, find it, and what I hear is the dialling tone. And then it rings again. It is the door. I switch on the lamp over the bed and look at the clock. It is not six, it is one. I pull my jeans on and a T-shirt, go out into the hall and open the front door. There is no-one there so I walk barefoot across the hallway, past the letterboxes, and then I see the Kurdish family from the second floor standing beyond the outside glass door in the cold. Three children: two girls, and a little boy crying quietly. The mother stares at the ground with her headscarf right down over her forehead, and though it is dark outside between the blocks, the light from the stairway shines red and blue and yellow in the flowers on her scarf, and the father with the big moustache smiles, he points at the lock and is bleeding from a cut on his cheek. He is my age, maybe slightly older. I go to the door and hold it open until they are all inside, and then I lock it again. He takes my hand and says thanks. I point at his cheek and look as enquiring as I can but he just shakes his head and smiles. Nothing to worry about. Right. He wears a white shirt under his grey jacket, and there are spots of blood on the collar. It looks dramatic, as in a film. He puts his hand on my shoulder and I *feel* that hand, he says thanks again, and then he points at my bare feet. It is so cold on the floor I am curling up my toes. Smiling, he pushes me towards my door, and then he opens his arms and puts them around his family and leads them gently and firmly upstairs, talking in a low, intense voice in a language I do not understand. The little boy is still crying. They have only been here for a few weeks, but he has learned to say "thanks". That will come in handy, no question. They are from northern Iraq. That is all I know.

I stay at the bottom of the stairwell listening to his voice fading and their steps fading on the way up. I could have invited him in, he could have come down when the children were in bed, and we could have had a drink or a cup of hot chocolate if that's what he would prefer, being a Muslim, and we could talk about having a family, that it's not that easy, or we could talk of Saddam Hussein, anything he likes. Maybe he can speak German, I know a bit of German, more people than you'd think know German, and the last thing I hear before the door slams shut two floors up is the boy crying loudly. With no stranger watching he doesn't hold back. Silence settles on the stairwell, and it is very cold. Beneath my thin T-shirt the elastic bandage is tight and uncomfortable, and I shiver uncontrollably.

It wasn't lung cancer; I had two fractured ribs. Not until I got home from town and walked, half bent over, past the mirror in the hall did I notice that I had a black eye as well. Everyone on the train and on the bus from the station had seen it, people I know and have said hello to for several years, only *I* didn't know. All the pains had converged into one big one, and I could not distinguish one from the other. And then I lay in bed, for days and nights, head spinning, before I called the doctor, dizzy from the want of air and thoughts of death, trying to unravel what had happened when I was far out of this world.

I go into my apartment and shut the door. Only the light over my bed is on. In the bedroom I ease one of my father's old sweaters over my head, it is washed out and soft to the touch, and then I put socks on before turning out the light, walking through the dark hall to the living room and turning on the lamp over the desk. The first thing I did when I found myself alone was to move the desk into the living room. There are two books on it and about a hundred pages of manuscript with a coating of dust on the top sheet. NEW BOOK is written under the dust. I find my cheap spare glasses, turn on my veteran Mac and click my way to the program I use now, then open a new file. I write:

"Early November. It is nine o'clock. The titmice are crashing against the windowpanes. Sometimes they fly unsteadily off after the collision, at other times they fall to the ground and lie floundering in the fresh snow before they get back on the wing. I do not know what I have that they want. I look out of the window across the field to the woods. There is a reddish light above the trees towards the lake. The wind is getting up. I can see the shape of the wind on the water."

I am writing myself into a possible future. Then the first thing I must do is to picture an entirely different place, and I like to do that, because here it has become impossible. And then there is a ringing. I look into the hall to the door, but this time it is the telephone. It is almost two o'clock. It is my brother. He is three years old than I am, a partner in a firm of architects, making money.

"Hi," he says.

"Do you know what time it is?" I say. "It's Tuesday, damn it, or it *was* Tuesday. Don't you have to work tomorrow?'

"Hi," he says.

"Hi. Are you drunk?"

"Not quite. Not quite yet . I think I'm going to be divorced."

"Oh boy! Welcome to the club. Does Randi know?"

"She's the one who knows. She hasn't told me yet. But soon she will. She's not here. I'm alone."

"Hey. Really. Who had long hair first? I did. And who cut it off first. Me again. I was the one to stick Mao on the wall, and I was the one who took him down again. I liked Bob Dylan first, and I liked opera best, and Steve Forbert I liked first, and the Smiths and Billy Bragg, and I was the one who said Ken Loach would be important, and now you don't watch anyone else's films. I read *Pelle the Conqueror* first, and I read *The Arch of Triumph* first and went to the off-licence to ask for calvados, and it cost more than 200 kroner, in 1973! I was the one who first went to a Vietnam demonstration. By the time *you* came along the war was almost over. I was married first and divorced first. You beat me by three days with the first child, but that was because I used condoms longer than you did. Maybe you'd never used condoms. Hell, you're three years older than me. You ought to come up with something I haven't already done. You could start to paint again, only you know how to do that."

"That's a lot of balls, I could make just as long as list. And anyway, I knew Dad better than you did."

"Why do you talk about him now? Christ, *Dad*. Why do you say *Dad*? Isn't is *Papa* any longer? We've always said *Papa*."

"*You've* always said Papa."

"Oh, no, I didn't."

"Listen, Arvid. Remember when we got back from Copenhagen after laying the wreaths on the sea along with all the firefighters and policemen and psychiatrists and priests, the whole shebang; and we went straight to Harald and borrowed his blue van and drove to Veitvet and stuffed it full of things from the flat. And then we went off again, to Gothenburg to cross with the ferry one more time with all the stuff we didn't actually know why we were moving, and we were so bushed that we fell asleep at the wheel before we had gone an hour so we had to stop at a Wayside Inn and flop on the benches outside, and I asked you if you felt guilty about Dad. You almost fell off the bench even though you were so tired."

"What are you talking about? I didn't fall off the bench. I thought we were talking about divorce."

"I'm talking about divorce. I have no idea what you are talking about."

"Don't talk to me about divorce. Shit, I know all about divorce."

"Right, that's good," he says, and hangs up, and I sit there with the phone in my hand, and then I hang up too, and the night is quiet again. It is dark in the hall, and it is dark outside, there is only light in one window in the next-door block. Mrs Grinde lives there. The neighbours say she has binoculars, and it may be so, I don't know anything about her, but she cannot be using them now, not unless they are army ones, and I do not think they are. I read the words on my screen: "I see the shape of the wind on the water." Did I write that?

I didn't make a speech on my father's seventy-fifth birthday. I had nothing against making a speech, but it did not occur to me for a moment that I should. We didn't make speeches in my family. Not for birthdays, not for confirmations, never had any one of us risen at the table to pay tribute to another. With a single exception. The previous year my mother had been sixty, and I gave a long speech in verse from all her children. I think she liked that, and I think she felt that at last they were getting some dividend for voting Labour and being loyal union members most of their lives so that we should have a better and richer life. It was a fine speech, and although it might not have won me the Nobel Prize for Literature I was quite proud of it. So on my father's seventy-fifth birthday I realised she was sitting there staring at me across the table. Dinner was well advanced, I was expecting nothing but peace, so I returned her gaze, and suddenly I realised that she was waiting for the speech I would be making for my father, and her expression told me she was really wondering what had I thought up this time.

I had not thought up anything. Nor could I spontaneously stand up and invent something. I had nothing to say. I turned and looked at the others at the table, my two brothers who were still alive and all the children and uncles and aunts, and they were all looking at me. The only one who was not looking at me was my father. And suddenly silence fell at the table.

I get up from the desk, walk into the hall, open the door to the stairwell and listen. I take a few steps, lean over the banisters and gaze up. Not a sound. It is the middle of the night, but maybe someone is standing up there and not moving. I clear my throat quietly, but the sound comes out loud and makes an echo and that is embarrassing, and I go in again to the dark hall and close the door. The two rooms next to my bedroom are empty now, but the doors are open, and it is dark in there too and not as before when at least one of the two girls had to sleep with a spotlight right in her face, yellow light under her eyelids and on into her dream. Now they do that in another place, another man maybe turns on those lights. I close both of their doors. Then I go into the kitchen. I won't be able to sleep anyway, I may as well have some coffee.

When my brother and I drove on from Vestby Wayside Inn that early summer of 1990 after the journey to Copenhagen when we had tossed wreaths on to the sea and drunk toasts in the bar with police inspectors, psychiatrists, firefighters and danced with nurses more attractive than we had ever seen before, we were really in trouble from lack of sleep, we had probably only had half an hour on the benches outside the inn, and that was far too little, but the sun was baking and it was impossible to lie there any longer. The van was hard to drive, at least for me it was, its gear lever on the steering column, which I wasn't used to, and anyway I hadn't driven a car for a long time. By the time we reached the Swedish border I was so tired and frustrated, getting into second every time I meant to be in fourth, that I let him drive the rest of the way to Gothenburg. He did so gladly. After all, he was Big Brother and I was Little Brother, and it was *his* neighbour who owned the vehicle.

"I envy you being able to put words to all that has happened," he said as we swung into the bend past the Lysekil turn-off, where we had been a few weeks before when the burning ship had been towed in to the nearest harbour, with hoses spraying from a retinue of fireboats, and we stood on the quay and looked up at the empty hull lying under a blue sky with great fan-shaped black patches around the portholes, and a policeman wouldn't let us go on board. It was Sunday and there were tourists there and people walking and small boats with dazzling white sails on their way out of the harbour, but no-one looked at the ship except us, and we started to argue with the Swedish policeman there on the long wharf, for we had driven so far, and we did want to go on board, but it was no use, and then I started to cry and I wanted to go for the policeman. My brother held me back and whispered something in my ear, I cannot remember what, but I went back to the car without resisting. Then we just sat in our seats and looked out of the windows.

He was wrong. I was body only and no words, just as he was, and no matter how much we talked there was always air between what we said and what we did. It was like champagne. I had tasted champagne at a publisher's party some time before and could get my name wrong when someone asked me who I was. Almost everything we said was wrong.

What we did was drive. We drove the whole time, we spent thousands of kroner on petrol. We couldn't sit still. We dived under the spaghetti junction on the way in to Gothenburg, and when we came out of the tunnel we drove straight into a wall of water. The rain poured down harder than we had ever seen, it slammed on the roof of the car and streamed over the windscreen and we couldn't see a metre in front of us. The world was glittering and milky-white and impenetrable with red dots that grew and grew, and I shouted: "Brake," and my brother hit the brake. The vehicle in front was suddenly dead ahead with huge rear lights. It was a massive trailer, stock still in the middle of the 70 limit, where it had given up. My brother stood on the pedal and spun the wheel at the same time, the car swerved and ended up crosswise on the road with the door on my side slap up against the back end of the trailer. T.I.R. it said in huge letters above the number plate.

I started to laugh, hit the dashboard with my palm and said: "A split second more and the whole Jansen family would have been wiped out. Not bad, that two months, and all gone. Some disappearing act."

My brother sat with his forehead on the wheel, and didn't feel like laughing, but then he had to, and then he cried a while, and then it stopped raining. Quite suddenly.

For the rest of the way to the boat we drove in silence, with the new light coming in through the windows, past the bridges and the steep wall of rock on the left, and turned off where the old America boats had moored, and the emigrants went on board with their chests and trunks for third class right down into the bowels of the ship, and had there been a car deck in those days, it would have been *under* the car deck, in cramped quarters with no other light than a dim bulb in the bulkhead, and what hope had left them. The sea sparkled, flat calm in the sunshine, and from Stigberget the remains of the shower came, as if from an unknown lake, in waterfalls down the long staircases and streamed out across the asphalt so the spray leaped up from the wheels of the van.

The crossing only took three hours. We could have sat in the saloon and read the bulky Swedish and Danish papers as we usually did, but we were drained and hungry and went straight to the restaurant. We ordered a three-course meal with beer and schnapps although before we had always just gone to the cafeteria, and we paid by Visa cards which were furry with insurance money. We spent two hours eating, and the third one we sat on deck in low chairs with our backs to the land we were approaching. A man stood at the rail gazing into the water. He didn't move an inch the whole time I was there, and I thought of maybe getting up and going over to stand there with him, but I never found the energy.

It was evening when we drove ashore, a light evening with warm sea air over the docks, and we drove through the harbour with the windows open and past the new railway station where the goods wagons lay in tight rows on the rails with rusty red fittings and Carlsberg painted on their sides in green. Outside the rebuilt merchant navy college a white-painted container crane stood on the lawn looking like something from a science-fiction movie. We drove north on the coast road with marram grass along the asphalt the whole way and the sea to the east and the sandy shore right down where we once found a dead seal, and the island with the lighthouse furthest out without its beam now for all we could see, and then on for the last bit where the gravel crunched under the tyres and the *rosa rugosa* bushes scraped our paintwork at the first turn. It was never going to get dark that evening, only the slanting half-light and the rows of shining seagulls in the shallows as far as the eye could reach. We turned into the avenue of willow trees, drove to the end and parked by the wall, switched off the engine and sat there saying nothing. The cabin was newly painted yellow, the light in the west behind it and the windows darker than everything else around us. A pheasant strutted across the lawn and into the field beyond. My brother watched it go, biting his lip, and I said: "We forgot to buy booze on the boat."

"Damn," my brother said. "That's true. That never happened before. And me dying for a drink. I've been thinking of it the whole way from the harbour."

"Me too. Maybe he's left a drop. He always buys it, but he doesn't drink much. Didn't, I mean."

We got out of the van, not slamming the doors but pushing them shut, because of the silence around us, not a sound but the sea sighing as it always does behind the trees by the shore when I realise *that* is what I can hear and stop thinking it is silence itself. My brother walked ahead with the key in his hand round the cabin to the door. He was more than ten centimetres taller than me and a good deal broader and was a buffer to the wind whenever it blew, while I walked behind, lighter on my feet and was ready to run if I had to.

It was colder inside than out. Two cups were on the worktop, and a half-finished crossword on the table. Time had come to a halt on the old ship's clock above the door, and my brother went from room to room mumbling: "Where the hell has he hidden the booze?"

I went out to the van and opened the back doors. A stove, a washing machine, several rag rugs, a couple of long shelves and a huge painting of a man smoking a pipe beside a house far into a Norwegian fjord. If I judged the perspective aright that man wouldn't fit into a house twice that size on his knees. It had hung on the wall above the sofa as long as I could remember, and we had always thought it was ugly. But it was an original painting, and my father wanted it there. It is *genuine*, he said when we were small, and that was something we could not argue with. No-one else we knew had a genuine painting on their wall, except Bandini across the road, but he made them himself, so that didn't count. I stood looking at all the things. There was a stove in the cabin already, and there was no room for a washing machine, nor plumbing for it. We knew that. I closed the doors and went inside again. My brother stood by the lavatory, saying: "I can't find the booze. I can't find the fucking booze."

"Have you looked in the bedroom?"

"Yes. In both cupboards. Nothing."

I went into the bedroom. It was like a double cabin. A bed next to each wall with a narrow gangway between them, and I recalled a joke I had heard in the Boy Scouts almost thirty years before. The Scout-master said: My wife wants two single beds because she needs something in between sometimes, and I want a double bed because I want to get my something between sometimes too, and I blushed as I would have done then if it had made any sense to me. I was ten years old and after four years at Sunday school, as innocent as a nun. I kneeled down and put my cheek to the floor and looked under my father's bed.

"It's crammed in here."

"With bottles?"

"No, with shoes."

"Get them out. Make it snappy," my brother said. He opened the window, he took the first pair and threw them on to the lawn. I heard them land and a shiver ran down my spine. I crawled further in and lay flat under the bed and pulled the shoes out, one pair after another, and some of them were old and some were brand new and had never been used. There was a strong smell of leather under the mattress there, and I recognised that smell from when I was small, on my way down the dimly lit stairs to the cellar where he stood at his workbench with rough leather in his rough hands and shiny tacks in his mouth, the yellow light and eerie shadows, and I do not know *what* we were up to, my brother and I, but I could not stop. My chest was bubbling, I felt like singing. I lay on my side and chucked the shoes as hard as I could along the floor, and my brother fielded them and hurled them on out of the window. At last there was nothing left under the bed. There had been twenty-five pairs in all, I had counted them, and every one was welted. He would never wear anything else. He hated cheap shoes. I backed away from the bed, stood up and went to the window and looked out. They lay on the lawn in a heap looking like something in a picture from Auschwitz.

"Did you find anything?" my brother asked. I blinked in despair and stared at him, and then I realised he meant the liquor. I had forgotten about that. I lay down again and looked. All the way in beside one leg lay a full bottle of Famous Grouse. I grabbed it by the neck and crawled out with my behind in the air, proudly holding up the bottle.

"Yess. I knew it," he said.

But of course it was *I* who had known, and for a second I felt completely without hope and did not understand why we were there just then, that I should not drink, it was the wrong moment, but I wanted a drink so badly. We went into the living room and I put the bottle on the table. He fetched glasses from the cupboard over the worktop and what was left in a litre bottle of Farris water we had bought at Svinesund on the border with Sweden. The fridge was still on, there were ice cubs in the freezer and a lonely Toblerone on the bottom shelf. He poured two stiff shots, then filled up with ice and a drop of mineral water.

"Skål," my brother said, raising his glass. I gripped mine and took a big gulp, staring at the oilcloth thinking I wanted an end to this, I couldn't take it any longer. I did not want to think about it any more.

But that's what I am doing now. I rise from the table with the cup of coffee in my hand, walk over to the window and look out into the dark. I have been far out of this world, I do not know where, and now I am back, and I can't stop thinking. I remember my thirty-fourth birthday in that very room, in the cabin where my brother and I sat drinking, in the far north of Denmark. It was four years earlier and darker then at the end of July, the bottles were on the table, and the lamps shone on the windowpanes. It was warm even though the door and several windows were open. I sat rocking on a chair in only a T-shirt, with my back to the kitchen counter. My mother and father had been there for several weeks, my brothers had come with their wives and children and sleeping bags and lilos. Not because it was my birthday but because it was summertime, and it was no longer a secret that a writer was what I wanted to be. My first story had been published in a magazine no-one had heard of before, but they had all read it anyway and were a little confused and uneasy because it was about my father. No-one was divorced yet, no-one had died, we went by boat as we had always done and slept through a familiar night. Lanterns and lighthouses lit our way from the fjord across the open sea and down past Skagen. Behind the boat the strip of wake lay foaming white and lifeline-like until it disappeared into the darkness. Now my father sat in a corner drinking. I had not seen him drink before. Not like that. We had not seen each other for a long time. He seemed smaller than before, but he was still strong, and I don't think there was a time in my life when he couldn't beat me with one arm tied behind his back. But he had never hit me, I had never even had a slap on the cheek except the once when he was trying to teach me to box and I refused to hit him and he became so annoyed that he slammed me on the chest and I fell over and landed on the floor and rolled under the sofa.

He stared into the glass in his hand, then rose unsteadily and said: "Well, well, Hemningway, so you're a writer." He didn't look at me but past me at something on the wall, or maybe he looked through the wall, and he smiled with his mouth only. I didn't like that smile. He wanted me outside with him, I realised that, but I didn't want to go. I was happy where I was, and so he went out alone. He had forgotten the cabin was a new one with an inside toilet, so he went outside as he had always done, across the lawn to the little outhouse and round the corner to the gap between the wall and the fence along the field. I saw his back in the dusk. Maybe it wasn't that strong any longer. He leaned heavily against the wall before straightening up, swaying a little, and trying to lean back again. But then his body sailed in the opposite direction, and he lurched out to steady himself with his hands, clutched the fence and slipped before he had a good enough grip and clung there until he got his balance back. Then slowly he straightened himself and let go of the fence. I didn't give it a thought until he came in again. That the fence was a barbed wire fence. His arms hung straight down and both palms were covered with blood. I was the only one who saw it. The others were chatting and laughing and celebrating my birthday, but between him and me there was a tunnel of silence. He paid no attention to his hands, just looked at the wall behind me and smiled in the same way and said: "Well, well, Hemningway, so you're a writer. Good for you."

I didn't know what to say. "Yes," I said, but that wasn't much, and no-one could hear it anyway. He stopped by his corner, picked up his drink and emptied what was left. When he put it down there were red smears all round the glass.

"We must have some beers, Hemningway," he said, and he turned on his heel and almost fell over, and then he walked across to the door, with full concentration, and went out and around the corner. The Tuborg bottles we kept in an outhouse called the Pigsty because it was used for pigs when we first came here. The outhouse was built of brick and we had put electricity in to keep two fridges going. To get there he had to go around the cabin and across the lawn. He walked close to the wall to support himself in the dark, I watched him through the curtain going past the big window, and then he disappeared from view and then I heard a thud. The others stopped talking for a moment and looked around before going on with their conversation. I sat waiting. After a while he came back with a bag full of bottles. His hands were still bloody and he was bleeding from a fresh cut on his forehead. The new windows tilted straight out, he had not seen them in the dark. The blood ran along his eyebrow down over his cheek and dripped on to his shirt collar. He was still smiling, rather stiffly now, and the room fell silent, everyone looked up, and yet only he and I were there. As he passed me on his way to the kitchen nook, he narrowed his eyes before he glanced sideways down at the chair I sat in and said: "Now then, Hemningway," and then he stumbled over the rag rug. The bag of bottles hit the bench and there was a sound of glass smashing. It was a film in slow motion. I saw his face on the way down, an incredulous expression in his eyes, before he landed flat on his chest with the bloody hands out to his sides. Now he will die, I thought. Everyone shot up from their chairs and the chairs crashed over, and I didn't want him to die, but I couldn't get up. I sat glued to my chair. I saw him lying with his back on the floor between the worktop and the wall and the beer running out of the bag over the newly varnished floor towards my chair. It was so hot in the room that the air turned misty and then into fog, and I saw everything through that fog: the furniture, the orange oilcloth, the photographs on the wall with the whole family history, curtains and lamps and my father on the floor in a lake of beer, and I didn't want him to die, I wanted to be ten years old again and have the smell of leather tickling my nose on my way down to the cellar, I wanted all that I looked upon to have a meaning and to surround and embrace me, and all that had happened to be gathered into one *now* and give me peace. I wanted my father to say Hemingway, not Hemningway.

But he didn't die then. He rose to his knees and impatiently pushed away the helping hands.

"Cut it out," he said. "This is nothing." He stared at the floor and said: "Isn't that so, Hemningway," and he was right about that, and then four years went by in which everything changed. Now only my brother and I were left. We sat drinking at the same table in the same room. We drank far too much, he said skål all the time, and we were going to get drunk. I took gulp after gulp and swallowed away as if drinking was the only thing I wanted in this world, and I felt anger coming, and I looked around me and said: "Wait a bit. Hold on a moment."

It was those photographs on the wall. I couldn't stand looking at them. And it was the curtains and the orange oilcloth and the knick-knacks on the window sill by the kitchen corner, it was the souvenirs from Germany and the journey to Siberia. I put my glass on the table, walked rapidly out to the car and found a roll of black plastic sacks behind the driving seat and went in again. I pulled off the first sack and started to tear at the curtains. They didn't want to come down. I took a good grip with both hands and leaned on them with all my weight. The loops tore and broke off the rail right over to the wall, and I went down and landed on the floor in a heap of striped cloth.

"For fuck's sake, can't you give me a hand?" I struggled up on all four. My brother got up from the table.

"What are you playing at?" he said. I didn't reply, just tore off another plastic sack and threw it to him and stuffed the curtains into the one I held. I pointed around me and he watched my finger and saw what it pointed at.

"You're crazy," he said. But he opened the sack, pulled the cloth off the table and fed it in, went across the room and took one photograph off the wall, and then another, and pretty soon there were none left, he was efficient, and I went to the window sill, and with my underarm swept everything on it into the sack with the curtains. In no time we had cleared the room, the sacks were full and we carried them out to the heap of shoes and left them there.

The cup is half full. The coffee has gone cold. I don't know what I have been doing. It is still dark, it is still winter, there's a cold draught from the balcony door. In the next block Mrs Grinde has put on her kitchen light again. It has been off for a while. I look at the clock. It says four. What is she doing up now, there's no-one to spy on except me, and I'm not that interesting, or maybe I am, to her, and I picture her even though I have only ever seen her out of doors, on the way to the bus or at the Co-op; the stern eyes behind her glasses, her small body restlessly passing from room to room, one lit, one dark, then one lit again, in her dressing gown maybe, her brown hair gathered at the neck in a rubber band, and the binoculars on the window sill.

I don't know. I get up, take the cup and go into the kitchen, pour the coffee down the sink, rinse the cup in hot water and dry it on the dish cloth. Then I hurl the cup as hard as I can down into the sink. It breaks with an unexpectedly loud crash. Some of the pieces fly over the edge and land on the floor. I pick them up and put them into the sink with the others, take a bottle from the worktop and start to mash all the pieces, it makes a horrible noise, but I don't stop until the cup has turned into a coarse powder. When I turn the taps on full, everything disappears down the drain. I suddenly hear myself breathing heavily through my nose. It sounds silly. I turn the taps off and all is quiet. Water has splashed up from the sink on to my sweater and my stomach is quite wet. I go to the cupboard in the hall and find another sweater, it is my father's too, I have four of them, and then I hang the wet one over the edge of the bathtub to dry. I straighten up and look at my face in the mirror. There is still a swelling under my right eye, but it is much less now, the colour more purple than blue and not so obvious, no longer the first thing you'd notice. That's what I think, anyway, but I don't really know, I haven't been out for almost a week, nor have I talked to anyone except the doctor and my brother and the Kurd on the third floor, and that was hardly a conversation.

I go on looking at myself in the mirror. I am so like him it would make you laugh. It won't be long before I reach the point where he was when I remember him way back, and I remember him well. If I screw up my eyes and stand there in the charcoal-grey sweater with the red band at the neck it looks like a photograph slightly out of focus from 1956. He was still boxing then. He was the eldest father in the block where we lived, but none of the others looked like him, at least not in the summer, in his shorts and nothing else on the lawn beside the road when there was voluntary work and a new path to be laid with flagstones, or when the balconies were being built and the whole house was out and there was not room enough for everyone in the photographs that were taken. We were twenty-five children and sixteen adults in eight apartments, there were bodies everywhere, white skin to the throat and sinewy arms, shabby belts and braces stretched like guy ropes over beer bellies, there were grazes on knees and spiky hair, there were big hands with crowbars and sledgehammers, and you could go wrong, you could pick the wrong parent, a sheepdog was needed to separate the families in the evening. I was the only one that never went wrong, for I always knew where he was. He was *visible*. In real life. In photographs.

I pull the sweater off and the T-shirt and stand in front of the mirror half naked with the bandage round my chest, and I still look like him. I am not like him, I smoke and drink when I feel like it, and I often feel like it. On Sundays I sit at home reading whether it's sunny or raining or snowing. I haven't owned skis since I was thirty. But I have trained for several years, sometimes a lot and sometimes less, I have lifted most things around me, chairs and tables and boxes of books, ten-kilo sacks of potatoes I have bought, I've stood in the kitchen and just lifted them; shopping bags full of milk cartons, I've lifted them up and down, up and down until the sinews by my wrists have tensed like bowstrings. I have attended health studios for six months at a time, and if I need to go to the shopping centre three kilometres away I walk, and I walk fast. All the way along the footpath past the football pitch, past endless rows of housing blocks and past roundabouts and two schools and a new sports ground and on down past the houses in Station Road which have been there for thirty, forty, maybe fifty years, to the centre beside the old E6, and then back again at the same pace up all the hills and especially the last one which is so long and steep that the breath burns in my throat and the lactic acid bubbles in my thighs right up to this satellite town at the north-east end of the Østmark Forest. When I get indoors I set the shopping bags on the floor and breathe like a man coming up for air before I do twenty push-ups in the hall, and then twenty more, and there is not one sweater that belonged to him that I cannot fill today.

I dress again and go to the telephone in the living room and stop and stand still. Then I lift the receiver and dial my brother's number. I let it ring five times before I put the receiver down. He is probably sleeping now, heavy as a soaked mattress, his brain swaddled in black velvet, and Randi is in town and won't be home until she knows what she wants, and he just has to wait.

I am not breathing so heavily any more. I circle the floor a few times and suddenly I feel fine. I take Svante Foerster's *The Class Warrior* from the bookcase and lie on the sofa to read it again. It is two years since the last time, and that's a long enough wait. I read the first sentences, and they feel as right as ever and my expectations rise. But I'm tired too, and the book is heavy, it is a big memorial edition with beautiful typography, and my thirty-kroner glasses make my eyes swim. I lay the book down on my stomach for a moment thinking that maybe Mrs Grinde is looking at me through her binoculars now, that I ought to do something indecent, and then I fall asleep.

3

There is a ringing and I wake up. It is the front doorbell, I realise that straight away. I'm lying on the sofa. I look at the clock on the wall. It says eleven. I have slept for more than six hours and I've dreamed about him. I know I remember the dream, that it is inside me perfectly clear and plain, that I can watch it like a video, but then the bell rings again.

It is light outdoors and light indoors, I've got my thirty-kroner glasses on my nose, *The Class Warrior* is on the floor. I sit up and rub my eyes hard. That hurts, I had forgotten about the swelling. Damn, I say aloud and pick up the book from the floor and put it on the coffee table and go through the hall to open the door. It is the Kurd from the third floor. He stands there smiling.

"Hi," he says in good Norwegian. It is a short word, though, about the same as "Thanks," I could have managed that too, in Kurdish or whatever his language is called, if someone instructed me first. I feel suddenly shy, I haven't quite woken up yet, I don't know what to say.

"Hi," I say. He holds something under his arm, a

41

small parcel. He gives it to me, I don't get the point, is it meant for me? He nods.

"Thanks," he says, but it is I who should say thanks, if the parcel is for me, so I too say: "Thanks," and then he smiles even more, and we stand there with our two short words, his cut on the cheek and the remains of my black eye, and have a conversation. Suddenly I am not shy any longer, I start to laugh, and we both laugh. I open my door wide and invite him in using international body language: fling my right arm out and make a slight bow, but then he laughs again and raises his hands palms outward and shakes his head. He points up the stairs, he has a family waiting, and in fact I don't mind that because I'm not too sure what state my flat is in. He raises his hand in farewell and says: "Hi," and I do the same, raise my hand and say: "Hi," nodding. I have understood, the little gift is for last night, because I interrupted my sleep to let him and his family in when he stood outside in the cold, bleeding, so far from the high mountains of Kurdistan with the moon so close and the deep valleys with their winding roads of fine-cut chippings and the good neighbours in white-painted houses with no locks on the doors.

He starts to go upstairs. The sound of his steps is one I already know, on the way up.

"Thanks," I say, waving the little parcel, and he turns and smiles and says: "Hi."

We cannot take it any further, there is nothing more

to say. I close the door and walk through the hall to the living room and sit on the sofa. I unwrap the parcel and put it on the coffee table. It is a small dish, a very shiny brass bowl with a design I imagine is Arabian or oriental at least, I'm really no good at the art of ornamentation, it might be Inuit for all I know. The famous Inuit brass artefacts.

I go to the kitchen and look into the cupboard and find two apples in a plastic bag. The skins are wrinkled, but they still have some colour and I go back and put them in the bowl and place *The Class Warrior* close to it. Two Norwegian apples in a bowl from a far country and a thick Swedish book on a white table. A still life from the home of a healthy intellectual, a man who has travelled the world. I sit there gazing. Two apples seem a little cramped, so I take one out, but that looks odd. I take them both away, roll a cigarette and light up, and as I smoke I tap the ash into the bowl. When the cigarette is half smoked, I stub it out in the middle of the oriental pattern. That really seems wrong. I have been given a present, and then I stub out my fag in it. I go back to the kitchen with the bowl in my hand, hold the stub under running water to be certain it's extinguished before I throw it in the bin, then I rinse out the bowl and polish it with the dishcloth. It is *not* an ashtray. I put the bowl in the middle of the kitchen table. It may shine there in the light from the overhead lamp.

I go into the bathroom and undress, take off the bandage and have a long shower. Then I turn off the taps, dry myself slowly, wipe the steam from the mirror with the corner of the towel and study my face. Not so bad. There is a stick of make-up in the medicine cupboard left by someone whose face I have forgotten, who doesn't need make-up any more because her face has gone, like the years have gone when I saw nothing except that face. I rub the stick lightly once or twice over the purple stain under my eye and spread it evenly with a fingertip. It looks almost natural. Perhaps I have just been sleeping badly, one eye open, always on the watch, as a writer should be.

I slam the door from the outside for the first time in a week. As I walk across the stairwell past the letter boxes on my way out, I hear a telephone ringing. It is mine. I stop, turn round and wait before turning back and then I open the door to the walkway outside. It is not locked now, it's the middle of the day. The ringing goes on in there, but I have been at home for so long that whoever wants me could have called me before. I want to go out.

It is March. Cold sunshine over the roofs, wind over the hills, hard snow in the shadows between the blocks, and the banks of snow alongside the walkway to the Co-op are sunken and hard as bone. All else is bare and dusty dry, the air is like Perrier. It pricks and stings the throat. I cough and swallow air, housewives come out with children in warm suits, and I cough again. They stare at me. I slowly breathe and hold the air as long as I can, I restrain from coughing and just as slowly let the air out again. I feel their eyes and the wind on my back. I pull my collar up to the neck and walk between the blocks and past the Co-op and the bus stop, and on to the walkway slanting alongside the steep hill and the road where a blue bus changes down on its way up. Grey clouds sweep along high above the ridge. They block out the sun for a moment and pass on, their shadows travel along the edge of the forest above the fields towards the tall block of the Central Hospital down in the valley, and turn to yellow what was grey. I stop and stand still. I close my eyes.

There's a strong wind. I stand alone on the hillside. I don't know where I am going. This was not what I had expected, but I cannot go up again. So I go on downhill to the shopping centre by the main road, staring straight in front of me until I cross with the green light and walk between the cars ranked close in the car park, and in through the tall glass doors.

It is Wednesday and only one o'clock, but there are people in all the shops on the ground floor and in all the ones in the gallery on the first floor, and high up under the ceiling there are great blue-painted beams across the whole span with long rails where the big cranes moved back and forth when this was a steelworks. It seems a long time ago now, but it is only fifteen years. I knew people who worked here. Reidar did, but Reidar is dead. He too wanted to write, and he did in the end, and then he died. But we were everywhere then, we who wanted the world to be new; in factories, on building sites, in print shops and tram drivers' seats, we wanted to assault the Winter Palace in the light of Lenin, see our muscles swell in the glimmer of molten steel, hear the tigersaw howl in red forests and stretch cables and groan and vigorously sing like the Volga boatmen, da da daa da, haaa! da da daa da, haaa! We wanted light over the land, and even if the world was like we said it was, almost all we did was wrong, for in every living room the lamps were lit and the TV sets flickered far into the night, and the world grew newer than we had ever imagined. Now the steelworks is a shopping centre, and a stone's throw away was my father's last shoe factory, where he jumped when the boss said jump until the factory collapsed under the weight of cheap Italian shoes, and then nothing was left. But I did not see him, did not want to see him. I saw the thousands on their march to Jenan and Dimitrov standing up against Hitler, I saw the masses of Petrograd and Mayakovsky's posters. I saw the mountains of Albania covered with guns and draped in red banners, and compared with all that he almost became invisible.

I walk among the shops in the big hall as far as the patisserie at the other end and take my place in the queue for a coffee and Napoleon cake. You can say what you like about Napoleon, but he *could* make a cake, my father used to say, and that was about as funny as he could get. He really loved Napoleon cakes. So do I. I take my tray with the coffee and cake and walk towards a table where smoking is allowed, and as I'm about to sit down I remember the dream I was having before the Kurd from the third floor rang my doorbell.

In the dream it was Easter time. I was twelve. We had gone out to the cottage by the Bunnefjord, it was morning and the sun shone sharply on the bare birch crowns where the crows roosted in dark clusters. They were unusually big. We had heard them carrying on quite early, before we got up, and we could hear them still. All else was quiet. My brother and I had climbed the rocks along the fjord towards Roald Amundsen's house until we were stopped by a high wire fence running down the steep slopes from the gravel road and continuing several metres out into the sea. We could see the house through the fence some way up from the shore, pale grey and huge in the sunshine, and the windows were dark. Roald Amundsen had been dead for a long time, but the house was still there and had been renovated, and if you paid the entrance fee you could go inside and look at his books and all the maps and polar bear skins and maybe a few old anoraks, but we had never done that, my brother and I. I stuck my fingers through the holes in the fence and put my face to it and shouted up at the house:

"I don't give a shit about Roald Amundsen!" I heard the sound of my voice so clear and metallic and I knew that I meant what I said, and what I said was momentously new. Now we were free to do as we pleased. We could smell the melting snow and the heather and the sun-warmed pines. It was springtime. The ice had broken on the fjord, only last night big patches had opened and lay darkly where before there was white in white, and the whole time floes broke free and floated on the current towards Oslo, and some of them ran inshore and hit the rocks with heavy thuds we could feel in our bones before the current turned them around and sent them on. There was a light wind. We stood on the smoothly polished rock that sloped down into the water, looking out over the fjord with the sun on our backs and our backs to Roald Amundsen's house. It was cold and warm both. We waited. The first floe was too small. We helped it on its way with two long poles we had found in a pile beside the fence. The next one looked fine. Rough and massive, but it was too far out, it would drift past and hit the shoreline much closer to town, and then we pushed the poles out to bring it to a halt, and it slowed down and turned towards the shore, and my brother yelled: "Jump." And then he jumped, and I jumped after him. We landed on the floe which kept swinging and crashed into the rock with a boom, slid up the bare rock some way and then began to turn over.

"Fucking hell," my brother yelled.

"Fucking hell," I yelled and dropped to my knees so I wouldn't slide off the floe and into the icy cold water, and my brother did what I did. We shoved our poles against the rock and pushed as hard as we could. And we did it. The floe slid off with a scraping noise and was flat on the water again, and then we were safe.

"Ho," said my brother, smiling.

"Hoho," I said.

Clutching the poles, we cautiously stood up. The floe turned gently and now we could see Roald Amundsen's house from a fresh angle and on towards the end of the fjord, we saw the whole of the Nesoddland up to the tip, and the islands nearest town, we saw Holmenkollen ski jump on the ridge, and then we saw it all a second time. After circling around three times, we had been taken by the current so far along we could see the shoreline to the plot that was ours and the path from the jetty up the hill to the cottage where my father came running down in his T-shirt as if it was summertime. He was a fast runner for someone over fifty, and he shouted something we could not hear, for each time he opened his mouth the crows lifted from the trees, and the sound they made filled the air around us. I did not care. It was great to be standing on the floe. I had a clear view to all sides, and everything I saw was familiar and at the same time completely new, and it gave me such a weightless feeling that my stomach seemed to dissolve, and I would not mind standing on that floe for ever, rushing along with the current and seeing the places I knew as if for the first time.

When we passed the jetty my father had come right down to the shore. We could hear what he was shouting now, it was our names, but I did not recognise mine. It sounded like it, but it was not mine. We were far from land, and if he wanted to get hold of us he would have to swim, and that was his idea. He threw himself out, the water splashing from his body on both sides, but it was icy cold, I heard him gasp, and he had not come far when I saw his face go white and he had to turn back. Back on land he started to run back and forth along the shore, calling, water pouring from his hair, from his clothes, and I heard the crows and his cries at the same time, and it was the name that was not mine and goddamnit, goddamnit, and then he caught sight of the rowing boat lying upside down in the shelter of a rock. It had been there since the previous autumn, covered with a tarpaulin, and he tugged and pulled it to turn it over and push it down to the water, but I knew the oars were not there. They were in the storeroom under the veranda on two benches, so he would have to run the whole way up to the cabin and then down again, and it's hard to carry two long oars and at the same time run. By the time everything was in its place and he was out on the water, we would be off. I turned and stood there looking straight across the fjord to Oslo while the ice floe gently rocked, and my brother was staring stiffly back at the rowing boat and at my father, and I think perhaps *that* is the difference between my brother and me, that in spite of size and age he always looked back while I look straight ahead, and this is the way it always has been. Right up to now. I don't know what has happened. It was something to do with a face. I had never seen it before, I did recognise it, but yet as it comes to me now, the thought of it is unpleasant. Someone gave me a gin. I had had enough already, I see my hand around the glass, the glass is full, and then the whole time there was that face with staring eyes and mouth wide open, and someone standing on the stairs, screaming and breaking vases, and there were mirrors everywhere. Mirrors everywhere, and he was shouting at me, but I didn't know who he was. He was intimidating, he said things I did not want to hear, I had to defend myself. All the words I needed lay tightly in line, ready to be said. I would break him with words the way he was breaking vases, but nothing came out. My lips were numb, my tongue was stiff, and my words were the things being broken, one by one as I was about to say them. I felt myself getting furious, I still wanted to defend myself, but when I looked at that face, I feared for my life, and then I do not remember anything more until I stood in front of the door of that bookshop in the centre of Oslo where I had not worked for three years. I kicked the door, but no one came to let me in.

What was it that he yelled? I have it on the tip of my tongue, but I cannot get it out. And the dream was so real, everything fitted, everything was as it could have been except for the name that was not mine, and the crows. They were unusually big. But they did not scare me.

It's a lousy Napoleon cake. The cream should be a pale yellowish white and light, but this one is feverish yellow and sticky. I eat just the top and leave the rest on the plate. I ought to complain, hold the cake up in front of the lady at the counter and say: "This is a cheap imitation, I want my money back." But I have never done that. I have never complained about anything except badly written books and the world situation, and you don't get your money back when little Nepalese girls are sold by their families to brothels in Bangkok, or because the World Bank refuses to waive cruel loans to Uganda. On the contrary. And lousy books; they just look at you and say: "Why don't you write one yourself, then?"

That's what I've tried to do. Several times.

I stub out my fag in the revolting yellow cream and get up and leave. I could have stayed there for a while to see if Thor the poet from Skjetten would turn up on his bike as he often does at this time of day to get a cup of coffee when he's desperate with writer's block, which is often the case, and we could have talked about how hopeless it is, the path we have chosen and gossip over colleagues who may have received a big grant from the state or do not sell books at all, and why that isn't in the least odd. Instead, I go by the escalator up to the first floor and go into the bookshop to see what others are up to while I am stuck. That is not inspiring. The piles left over from Christmas are still there and have not diminished at all, and there are none of mine on the shelves. That is not so strange. It is more than three years since I last published anything, and the woman behind the counter does not recognise me although I have at least twice sat in front of that counter at a small table signing books. I remember myself at eighteen reading Keats and Shelley and Byron and dreaming of publishing *one* book, or maybe two, which would be on everyone's lips and be everyone's mirror, and when they looked in that mirror they would see the people they might have been and they would have to cry, and after that I would just disappear, become one of the young dead and thus immortal, but now I am one of the middle-aged forgotten. I enquire after the lady who runs the shop because *she* will know who I am, and we often have a chat. But she is in hospital with a stroke, she has lost the power of speech, the lady behind the

53

counter says in a confidential, solemn voice, without even recognising me, and then I ask if they have any books on Kurdistan or at least on northern Iraq, and she tells me I should go to the library. But I do not go to the library, I go home. That is, I go to the bus stop.

Several of the neighbours are there, standing in the queue, and then they get on the bus with me. They greet me warily. I nod and turn away and walk between the seats to the back, then sit down by the window and lean my forehead against the window glass. The bus starts, I feel a vibration in my chest, in my stomach and groin. Even since I was small I have ridden in buses with my forehead to the window and gazed out without really looking or thinking, just concentrating on the vibration in my body, until my body *was* that vibration, and when I get off it is like a sleep it hurts to wake up from, my skin electric and open to whatever may strike it and rip it to shreds, and yet the worst thing is when someone gets on that I know and sits down on the seat beside me with a big smile and wants to talk.

On my way in to the stairwell I hear the ringing again. I don't care, I don't want to talk to anyone. I open the letter box calmly and fish out *The Class Struggle* and a flyer from the Co-op and Rælingen parish magazine, and then take out the key and run to my door, fumble with the lock, swear out loud and run into the hall and pick up the phone.

"Just a moment," I say. I clutch the receiver to my chest and breathe heavily and hold a hand to my side, where it suddenly hurts. Maybe the doctor made a mistake, maybe it is not the rib, maybe it is something else entirely. Then I lift the receiver. It is Randi. Why doesn't my brother call himself, why is his wife calling?

"I've been trying to reach you all day," she says.

"You have? I have been out. I do sometimes go out, as a matter of fact."

"It's your brother. He's in the Central Hospital," she says, but that cannot be right, because I have stood looking down at that hospital today, and I should have felt something if he was there, but I did not feel anything.

"What's he doing there?"

"He's been admitted."

"But shit, I've just been talking to him."

"You have? When?"

"Last night. He called me."

She gets mad, she says something quickly, hard, but she doesn't speak into the receiver, so I do not catch it, and there is a silence; she is breathing, and I am breathing. I stand in front of the mirror in the hall. It is difficult to focus, but there is someone there, I've seen him before. I nod, and he nods, and then I recognise myself.

"So tell me what's happened."

"A bottle of port and a hundred Sarotex is what has

55

happened. A hundred Sarotex without capsules so they would work quicker. The capsules were in the bathroom when I came home this morning, and the bottle was in the living room, empty. I rushed all over the house, but I couldn't see him anywhere. In the end I found him in the shed. It was cold out there, Arvid, I don't think I can take this any longer," she says, and that's probably true. She starts to cry, and I wonder what the hell is Sarotex, and I try to remember when it was I last saw my brother, face to face, but all that comes to mind is that once we fought in the hall at home when he was twelve and I was nine, and we were alone and rolled on the floor and punched and punched each other and tore the coats down from the hooks and knocked the chest over and tipped the vacuum cleaner out of the cupboard which was open, and it burst apart and everything that was in it spilled out on the floor and made a massive cloud of dust and dirt, and then we suddenly stopped because we realised both at the same time that we hadn't anything to fight about. We never did have. And we were both so embarrassed that he went straight to his room and shut the door and I went out. I ran round the block the longest way and sat down under the poplars beside the dustbin where the blackbird used to sing, and I thought I had lost myself, that I did not know who I was, because I was the one who had attacked him, and I had no idea why.

4

When my mother and father came out of the tabernacle in Hausmannsgate after they had stood before the priest and both said yes, my father stared at the ground with a frown on his face, and turned to one of his brothers, Trond, and said: "Nailed to a cross on earth." And then he laughed.

I don't know how many people heard what he said, but *I* heard it from Uncle Trond on the telephone only a month ago, and you might think I would feel my father was a shit for saying a thing like that, for if anything I was a mother's boy, but I did not, I thought: Christ, did *he* say that?

It was October, it was sunny, and my mother had not learned to speak Norwegian yet, but she made herself perfectly well understood, and "ja" was more or less the same in Danish, so she got that right. She was slim again, or as slim as she could be. She had let her hair grow down to her shoulders after keeping it short for several years, and it was more curly now than frizzy, and she had a white flower stuck into it above one ear about where Billie Holiday used to wear hers, and like Billie Holiday she needed no clasp to fasten it with. She pushed it in and it stayed put. She probably needed that flower, for not one of her family was there in Oslo that day.

They all were on my father's side. Four brothers and two sisters and my grandfather Adolf Jansson, a Baptist from the countryside south of Sunne in Värmland, Sweden, who was finally award the King's silver medal of merit for long and acquiescent service at Salomon Shoe Factory, where he had been all his working life, where all his children worked, a factory he must have chosen because of its name or because the people who ran it shared his brand of faith.

Now they were clustered on the pavement. My mother smoked a cigarette, the only one who did, except for maybe Uncle Alf who had ambitions and wanted to leave the factory, and I do not know whether she took in my father's biblical sense of humour. Anyway, there was complete silence. She stood at the edge of the little group. A whirlwind spiralled in the grey street and lifted her hair, made it big and sparkling in the autumn sunshine, and her dress was pale blue and swung around her strong calves, and it looked like a dance, but I do not think she thought that was what she was doing. Dancing. Her hair settled again, and her dress fell into place, and she stubbed out her fag with the toe of her shoe on the side of a kerbstone, pushed a hand in under her blouse to straighten a bra strap, while my father looked the other way, while they all looked the other way, and then they went down the street to the photographer round the corner in Storgata.

I keep that photograph in a drawer, and it's just the two of them there, but I can sense the others, they push against the edges of the picture wanting to be in it, and my father likes that, I can see it by the way he smiles. He is at ease again, surrounded by his family, and as long as that lasts he does not have to think about how bewildering it is to find himself there at this moment. For a while it was difficult, but now they stand close, and he has a lady beside him with long dark curly hair. She is Danish. He does not know her very well. She looks obstinate, but she is good-looking in a southern way, like an Italian, or maybe Moroccan, and in the inside pocket of the jacket he fills to bursting point there is a picture of another lady who is Danish too, stuffed between the notes his father gave him for a wedding present. It is stupid and he knows it, but he cannot part with it, and in fact it is not that bad to stand shoulder to shoulder with one attractive lady and have another in his wallet. He thinks of that too as he looks at the photographer and faintly smiles.

The only one who is no way near the picture is my brother. He was put away on a farm belonging to someone my mother knew on an island off the coast of Denmark. There he trudged around among sheep and sheepdogs and thought that all was well with the world. He had very fair hair and was almost eighteen months old. I don't know how many knew he existed. My father knew, or he would not have been standing outside the tabernacle saying: "Nailed to a cross on earth."

My brother's hair is darker now, and thinner. He is forty-six. There is a tube in his mouth and another through his nose, and one is fastened to the back of his hand, and there is a screen by the wall where a curve moves up and down, up and down towards a point it will never reach, and it looks as though it moves a little unevenly, but then I don't understand such things. I pull a chair to the end of the bed and sit down. It is evening. As I walked down the corridor to ask my way, the nurse on duty stuck her head out and said: "That was none too soon."

"I couldn't get here before," I replied.

But that was not true. I had walked around the apartment for quite a while, and in the end I lay down on the sofa and fell asleep at once, and when I woke up it was far into the evening. I emptied a glass I had poured from a bottle I kept in the kitchen cupboard, brushed my teeth and then got dressed and left.

"I mean he survived by a hair's breadth. Half an hour more . . ." she said, leaving the rest to drift. "Are you family?"

"I'm his brother," I said. "I am the only family he

has," and even if that is not true either, the look she gave me made me so furious that I was still shaking as I went on down the corridor.

"He is stable now," she said icily behind me, but I did not turn round, merely found the right door and went into the intensive care ward and stopped by his bed.

I sit there for a long time just watching him. His eyes are closed. His eyelids are swollen as his face is swollen, and he looks big and seems immensely heavy beneath the thin duvet on the bed of this white-painted room. He was the first one in our family to pass his examination to go to university. He was the first one in our *street* to go to university. That's more than twenty-five years ago. I can remember the black student's cap that was kept tidily wrapped in soft paper on the top shelf of the cupboard in the hall, and he used it that once only, when he enrolled at the university, because it embarrassed him, but he thought he had to, and then he put it away for good. When I passed my student's examination three years later and enrolled at the university, it never occurred to anyone that I might want a student's cap. But then nothing came of it. I never showed up. I lost my courage, or something else was lost, and with my hand upon my heart I cannot say my father was sorry for it.

My brother's bare chest rises and falls slowly and

evenly and the graph makes the same movements on the screen, then he suddenly raises himself on his elbows and starts to speak in a language only drunk men understand. One of the tubes comes loose and falls onto the duvet, and he opens his eyes and looks straight at me.

"You're stable," I say. "Relax, for Christ's sake." But he does not relax, he starts to shout, and if the name he shouts is mine, I do not recognise it. I go and fetch the nurse. She lays her hand on his forehead and fastens the loose tube, and then he slides down on to the pillow again.

"He doesn't seem very stable," I say.

"He is stable, but he doesn't know you're here. If you come again tomorrow you may get through to him. He's full of poison now."

I feel offended on his behalf. "There's nothing the matter with my brother, he just can't stop looking back."

"Is that so?" she says, smoothing the duvet and straightening the tubes, and looking at the screen as she mumbles: "Of course he's stable," and then she says more audibly: "Do you want to sit here a while longer?"

"A bit longer, maybe." I sit down again and she leaves, and I sit perfectly still looking at him, and then I fall asleep, and when I wake up she is standing in the doorway. She smiles.

"I've made come cocoa. Would you like a cup? You can come along to the office with me."

I haven't tasted cocoa since I made a jug the morning my daughters moved out. It seems a long time ago. I say yes, please, and get up and follow her. The big hospital is quiet, there are thousands of people here, but they do not make a sound. Only one patient suddenly coughs behind the curtain in the corridor as I go by, and I try to walk without a sound in my lace-up boots, but it's not easy. In the nurses' office she pours me a cup, and I sit down on a spare chair drinking the hot cocoa slowly, letting it warm my stomach while she writes a report or whatever it is that nurses write at night. She looks up at me once or twice and smiles. I like her better now.

"It tastes good," I say, and she smiles and nods and goes on writing, and then I start to cry and get up with the cup in my hand and stand by the window until it has passed and then I sit down again and say: "He's going to be divorced, you know, but that's not what this is about."

Carefully, she puts down her pen and looks at me with absolute calm, and then I tell her about the boat and the fire and all those who died in the flames, and died from the poisonous smoke, and how they lay close together in the companionways, side by side like a single conjoined body, and many lay on top of their children to shield them from the smoke, and some were in the shower with the water running, and that did not help them at all, but there was nowhere else to go, and only those having a ball in the bar had all their clothes on, because it was the middle of the night, the way it is now. And she nods, she remembers that fire, *everyone* remembers that fire, that's why it is so difficult to talk about, they all nod and grow quiet, and it is like beating a duvet filled with down; completely numb and dumb, and they nod and nod, but she merely pours me a second cup of cocoa, and I drink it slowly, for it warms my stomach so pleasantly. I wonder whether it is proper cocoa or one that takes five seconds with a teaspoon and boiling water, because it reminds me of the kind my mother made when I was a child, and I look around for the packet to see what it says, and then I tell her of all the discussions we have had since then, my brother and I, about how they died, my two younger brothers and my mother and my father, and I have said it again and again, that they were asleep and died from the smoke and never knew what had happened to them, while *he* is convinced they were awake and tried to get out, and then could not because the flames were so fierce at that particular place in the boat and the smoke was so thick, and he cannot stop thinking about what their thoughts were just then, what their last feelings were, and I have said it does not do any good to go on thinking like that. "But he cannot stop," I say. "Six years have gone by, and goddamnit, he cannot stop thinking about it."

"Shall I make some more cocoa?" she asks, picking up the empty pitcher. For a moment I think that that would be great, and I could see how she makes it, and then just sit there drinking really good cocoa, but I do not say that, I say: "No, thanks, I'm fine."

She puts the pitcher back and looks out of the window down at Gamleveien where the line of street lights glitter, and then it is dark all the way up to the ridge where I live in an apartment block in a satellite town I usually call the Eagle's Nest.

"If he had succeeded in what he was trying to do, then you would have been left alone," she says, and my heart sinks, I know that song, I don't have to listen to that crap, and anyway it's not true, I am not alone, there are people in my life although none comes to mind at this very moment, but she may not be talking to me, as she is just sitting there looking out of the window, she may be talking to herself.

"I cope," I say. "I always have." I put my cup on her desk and stand up. She turns, but she didn't like that last remark, that's obvious. She does not want me to cope, she wants us to be dependent on each other and hold each other's hands and have dinner together every bloody Sunday and be a close and happy family with a summer house on the coast and have smiles on our faces no matter what happens. She belongs to the Christian People's Party, I can tell from her dialect.

"You want to look in on him again?" she asks.

"No, I'll come back tomorrow. Maybe he won't be so stable then."

She does not think I am funny at all.

In the lift going down there is a woman who cannot stop weeping, and I do not know which department she has left, maybe maternity a few floors up, where I have been twice in an earlier life, and if she comes from there and is weeping still it must be because she has a daughter of fourteen who has had her first baby and will not tell who the father is. Her tears trickle down her face and she looks at me as if I might say something wise at any moment, and that is what she needs right now, for me to say something wise to make her stop feeling such a lousy mother, but she has got the wrong man. I have nothing to say. At the ground floor I walk from the lift and can hear her behind me, sniffing all the way through the vast, empty entrance hall to the door.

It is cold outside, and immediately dark as I walk out of the ring of lights that circles the yard in front of the hospital. The ambulance helicopter is parked on a pad some distance away like an enormous insect with long shadows, and when I turn into the walkway to Gamleveien I hear a man shouting and motors starting up and the fluttering rush of the rotor blades, and I turn and watch the helicopter take off tail first and then rise in an arc around the hospital block and vanish high up over the ridge with its searchlights aiming for the Østmark and the great lake and the forests on the other side.

I come down to Gamleveien and walk alongside the lamp-posts up the first slopes which are not too steep, and it is dark on both sides, but I know how the fields undulate and rise to the right towards the ridge lying there huge and heavy, and I know how steep it is and dread the last long slope. Suddenly a car comes down the road. The headlights dazzle me so I have to stop and stand still for a moment, and as it goes past I see the compartment light is on. The car is crammed with people and they laugh, and one has a bottle in his hand, and they are all quite young. There is music howling from the car stereo, and the driver leans on his horn to greet me, a middle-aged man on his way through the night on foot, and they do not have a care in the world at this moment. I turn and watch the car with its lit interior and red rear lights until it disappears round the bend before the church and how it rushes past, and the last thing I hear is the bass thumping out through the half-open windows.

I walk on again. Everything is quieter now, the asphalt glittering with frost. I am freezing in my pea jacket, I put on speed and find a pace I can manage without exhausting myself. When I come to the foot of the last hill I am warm and sweating and a little mad, so instead of following the walkway along the ridge I take the path that goes up through the spruce trees, which is twice as steep but much shorter. Halfway up I have to stop. I do not know what is wrong. I cannot take another step. My legs are shaking and my side hurts. I lean against a tree practically panting, then lie down with my feet resting against the trunk to stop myself from sliding. Through the trees I see the lights of the hospital in the valley and the street lamps along Gamleveien and otherwise nothing. I close my eyes, I hear the wind in the treetops, and it is a good sound. I have heard it both summer and winter on hundreds of cross-country treks with my father, when we rested and my breath was not the only sound I could hear, and sometimes the wind in the treetops was the only thing that *was* good. And sometimes it was good when he stood there on the ski track in front of us with his arms stretched out to his sides taking deep breaths and then keeping the air down for a long time, and letting it out again and passed it all on to us who were his sons when the hills were steep on the way up to Lilloseter and Sinober, deep into the forest. We stood there in a line, with our skis on whether we wanted to or not, our arms stretched out, with thick gloves and dangling ski poles, and he said: "Close your eyes, breathe deeply, and let the air out again slowly, and you will see that it helps." And we did that in chorus. Took deep breaths with loud gasps, and the forest that surrounded us grew quiet, and the world held its breath while we held ours, and when we let the air out again a wind came that lifted us all for years until it could carry us no more. And I never asked myself why, never looked back to find out whether he was still standing there, but now I am sitting in the middle of this steep slope on a ridge north-east of Oslo with my feet against the base of a spruce tree to stop me from slipping, and there is not much snow now, but it is well below freezing, and I stretch my arms out to the sides and suck the air in, keep it down for a long time and slowly let it out again, and I do it once more and then again until I find a rhythm I can keep. I gently pump *space* into my chest which has been cramped for a long, long time, until the silence inside me matches the silence that surrounds me. I lie down again with my back in the pine needles, and it feels good to breathe the ice-cold air. I look up between the tree trunks to the sky, which is completely clear and full of stars, and it slowly turns around, the whole world turns slowly around and is a huge, empty space. Silence is everywhere, and there is nothing between me and the stars, and when I try to think of something, I think of nothing. I close my eyes and smile to myself.

5

A roaring sound wakes me. I hear it from the inside of something which is not a dream, which is different from a dream, and the sound gets louder and louder, and I want it to stop, but it does not. A white crack opens and there is light streaming in, and even if I squeeze my eyes shut the light just gets stronger. The roaring sound pushes me down and fills my head, and then I have to open my eyes, and I see the helicopter's searchlight sweep down the ridge, and its rear lights, and the pressure of the air from the rotor blades makes the treetops above me thrash against each other. All the space around me undulates and swirls, and I am lifted up and sink again, like a carpet in *A Thousand and One Nights*, and it is night now, I remember that. And then the roar grows fainter as the helicopter follows the hill on its way down and makes an arc around the hospital block before landing, and then it disappears.

I lie perfectly still. I know I am freezing, that the cold is just about to grab me, but if I do not move I can keep it at bay, let it stay out in my body and away from that which is me. I could lie here like a Zen Buddhist bundle in a blue pea jacket and be pure spirit. That would have been something. But it won't work. Once I have thought of movement there is no way back. I *have* to raise my arm. And then I can't do it, the link is broken, I must concentrate and use all my will, and the moment I see my arm go up, I start to shudder. First in the hand, it vibrates, and then the arm vibrates, and it spreads to my hips and on to my legs and back again at full strength so that my teeth start to chatter and my head beats against the ground, there is epilepsy in all my muscles, and I let out a howl so horrible and cut up that I stop at once. Down there is the road, behind my head up the hill are the blocks of flats. Who heard me howl? There are wolves in the forest, bar all your doors.

I struggle to my knees, my body shuddering as if it knew no shame, there is ice in my spine and it is dark between the trees now the helicopter has gone, and the hill rises vertically before me. Then I get to my feet and start to climb. I do not know how long it takes me. But anyway it does not matter, for time is the same in both directions, and all is the same on my way up the hill, I could go on like this for ever. I take up lot of space and lose the path and bump into trees and stumble over stones, and I imagine someone standing there, looking at all this and laughing, for I am good entertainment. I would have liked to have seen me myself and I laugh too, between my chattering teeth. Ho, ho, ho, I laugh, ho, ho, ho, and suddenly I am standing close to the nearest block. Where did that come from? But it is not my one. They look alike, but it isn't mine. I have to go round this one and on past two more blocks, and then I am home. I can do that. I move on again, and finally get round the last corner. There is light in one window in the block up to the right. That is my window, and I stop and lean on my knees and I puff and I shake and I stare up at the window thinking: that is where I live. And I consider what I think of that, and then it all turns empty. In the block to the left there is light in a window right opposite mine, and Mrs Grinde is probably standing there looking across at me. But I am not home, I'm standing right here. And I shall stand here as long as I have the strength.

A lamp is alight above the door to my entrance. I take the last steps over there and suddenly it seems a nice light to me, a wonderful light, and with frozen fingers I fumble in my trouser pockets, searching for my keys, and then they are not there. But I always keep my keys in my right-hand pocket. I have travelled all over the country and in England and the USA and always kept my keys in the same pocket, for no matter how ingenious a place I find I always manage to forget where it is. But they are not in my trouser pockets, nor my jacket pockets, there are no keys in any pocket. I lean against the door. I am freezing. I look at my watch. It says half past three. I look at the doorbells and name plates by each bell push. His name has been written with a ball-pen on a scrap of cardboard. Naim Hajo. One favour is worth another, is what I think, about to press the bell push. But then I remember the brass bowl. We are quits, he does not owe me anything. Besides, he has children, it would wake the whole family. I can't do that, and I realise that even if I freeze until I can no long think I shall not ring that bell. So I go to the only place that comes to mind.

The door to her block's entrance is not locked, and the stairwell is painted the same as mine is, a cheerful blue in two shades in accordance with strict rules, with stencils of flowers on every third step to make it cosy, and it is so cosy that goose pimples spread on my skin as the cold strikes out from the walls, and it should have been spring now, but it is all a mess. I walk upstairs to the second floor of this stairwell that looks like mine but is not mine at all, and I push the bell where it says G. GRINDE on a small green plate above the bell, and I figure she must be called Gudrun Grinde, like an auntie on children's television, or Grete, or Guri, or Gunilla Grinde, maybe she's actually Swedish.

There is a long silence. I know she is there, but she does not come to the door. My legs are shaking, I can't stand up much longer, so I sit down on the lowest step of the stairs going up to the top floor facing G. Grinde's door and listen. Finally, I hear footsteps on linoleum, the door handle turns and the door slowly opens. Out sticks a mop of brown hair and a frightened face I have only seen in the shop and sometimes behind her window, but then she's had her glasses on. Her eyes are nothing like as severe as I remember them. She ought perhaps to change glasses or get herself some contact lenses. I can see the collar of a dressing gown, dark blue with red stripes, it is quite shabby, and I can see the skin of her neck in soft shadow. She stares at me blankly. Through the crack in the door I can glimpse the room that looks out on to the grounds and on to my block. There is a bed in there. It is not the kitchen. I do not know why I thought it was the kitchen. There is a light on by the window, and a coat-stand at the end of the bed. There are no binoculars that I can see.

"Did I wake you?" I say. And I suddenly realise I have done just that, but she makes no reply. She does not understand anything.

"I hope you were awake," I say, "I saw the light was on. It was the only light in the whole block, so I came here. I didn't know where else to go," I say, and as I speak I try to get up from where I am sitting without shaking. It's not so damned easy, and she swallows quite visibly, and then she says in a surprisingly deep voice: "I always sleep with the light on."

"Oh," I say, and her eyes slowly focus. Now she is really staring at me, she recognises me, and I am on my feet now, I am standing straight, if not steadfast. But my teeth are chattering.

"Hell, you'll have to forgive me," I say. "I don't know

what I'm doing. I saw the light was on, and I just came up here. That's all. I'm sorry to have woken you up. I'll go away now." And I start to walk, but I can't stop shaking, and there is a clattering in my mouth, that step I sat on was far from warm, and I must look pretty weird.

"Are you ill?" she asks.

"I don't know. I'm freezing, I can tell you that. I'm as cold as hell," I say, and laugh, "ho, ho, ho."

She is awake now, and my laughter confuses her. She bites her lip.

"So why are you so terribly cold?"

"I fell asleep down on the hillside. Luckily something woke me up."

"An angel, maybe," she says, and suddenly smiles such a sweet smile that I could have fallen to my knees and kissed her dressing gown, but that would have been way too much for me in the state that I am in, and certainly for her. She is younger than I had imagined, or rather, certainly younger than *me*, which is not saying much at present, for everyone I see these days who is definitely a grown-up is younger than I am, and it doesn't help no matter how long I look at myself in the mirror. I see the same person I have always seen, whereas everyone else keeps changing, and I have a shock each time I realise that this is not how it is.

There is a vein in her neck that pulses almost

unnoticeably. She doesn't know that herself, but *I* can see it and that is where I keep my eyes fixed.

"It was a helicopter," I say.

"A modern angel then," she says and laughs softly in her deep voice, and then I know I don't want to leave.

"Maybe it was," I say. I shiver and hang in there, she might laugh once more, she might ask me in, anything might happen on a night like this when no-one else is awake except perhaps a nurse who at certain intervals walks down a corridor to check a curve on a screen. I wish she would ask me in. I cannot just stand here indefinitely.

She bites her lip again and says: "Maybe you had better come in for a while. You don't look too well." She opens the door wider and steps aside. I can see into the hall and straight into the mirror hanging on the opposite wall. If that is me in the mirror by God I don't look well, my face white and unfamiliar, my hair sticking out in all directions and there are big stains on my jacket and the knees of my trousers. How does she dare, I wonder.

She keeps it nice and warm in her place. I feel it on my face as I cross the threshold. There is a chair just to the right of the door. I sit down on that. I do not want to intrude, I don't know *what* I am doing here really, it is just that I can't find my keys. But I have not told her that yet. She stands barefoot in the middle of the hall with a dressing gown tied tightly round her waist with a leather belt, like a paramilitary dressing gown, I think, and she runs her hand through her hair and bites her lip, and I close my eyes and let the heat ooze gently in through my clothes, through my skin until my hands and feet start to tingle so sharply that it hurts, and I could not have moved if I wanted to. But I do not want to. I want to sit right here.

When I open my eyes again she looks different. Her hair has been brushed back from her face.

"I can't see very well without glasses," she says. "I thought you were drunk, you frightened me a bit."

I nod. "I'm not drunk," I say.

"No," she says. "You're not drunk. I can see that now."

She stands short-sighted in front of me, and I sit on the chair. We are waiting for something. Here in the no man's land right inside her door; the to-and-fro place, but no place really. Finally, she sits down on the chest underneath the mirror. She is tired.

"Could I just sit here for a bit?" I say. "Then I'll go away. You go back to bed. I'll be fine."

She runs her hand through her hair. "Oh, but I can't do that," she says.

No, of course she can't. We wait again. She thinks my eyes are closed, and they are, in a way, at least very nearly, but I can see her all the same and I like her and I like the skin of her throat and know how warm it is just there and then on and on into extents and roundings beyond comprehension. But *she* doesn't know that, I can see she does not, and I would have to talk her out of that belt and that dressing gown and into her bed and then do what I had to do, which I honestly have nothing against, but really am not up to right now, to get into that warmth and thaw myself out as Erik Lagus did in the Stockholm of *The Class Warrior* thirty-three years ago when I was only ten and knew all there was to know about skin without even giving it a thought, for the warmth was everywhere then, in the walls of houses and rough stones and in the bark of the tall pine tree by the path down to Dumpa and in the hoods of black cars and in my father's blue T-shirt and what was inside that shirt. But all that was lost long ago, and I do not have the strength to try. It is hard work. It would take me at least an hour to get her there even if it was at all possible, and I only have a few minutes left before I must leave. It is too late now to say I have no keys.

I open my eyes wide, looking straight at her, and then she gets up from the chest, not impatiently, but restlessly maybe, at a loss.

"May I tell you something?" I ask.

"About what?"

"Something about my father."

She bites her lip again and does not know what to say, and then she says: "I suppose you may. Will it take long?"

"Oh, no," I say.

*

Only six months before my father died he had to go to
hospital. He had been there earlier for a minor
operation. Now they were afraid he had cancer. He was
seventy-six, but on the few occasions I saw him he
looked the same as he had always done. Maybe I was
being dim. I don't know. There were so many other
things. My head was full of cotton wool. I was always
tired. My first book had just been published. Almost
everything in that book was about him, and I knew he
had read it, my mother said he had, but he never
mentioned it when I went home to visit. Their
neighbours too had read it and the other old chaps
stopped him on the road in front of the house and said:
"Well, well, Frank, we didn't know you used to be such
a tough guy," and then he just smiled secretively and
would not say a word. Perhaps he was a little proud, or
he smiled because he had no choice. I will never know.
But he and I could not talk.

Then my mother called one day.

"Your father has been in hospital for several days,"
she said. "You have to go and see him."

I'm sure I knew he was there. One of my brothers
must have told me, but I hadn't taken it in. It was
nothing to do with me. I had never been to see anyone
in hospital before. But now I did go.

It took less than half an hour to drive to Aker
Hospital. It was early October and the rowan berries

hung in heavy clusters at the edge of the forest alongside Gamleveien on the journey in. All the leaves had blown away in a few nights, all the colour was gone, and the berries hung as the only decorations, and had ripened and fermented in the cold weather and were about to split, and I had heard the thrushes liked them especially just then. They gobbled them up and afterwards were so intoxicated they were not able to fly straight. They could not get enough of them. It's the truth. Someone I trust had told me, and that was what I was thinking about as I drove in to the hospital along Gamleveien, past Lørenskog station and on to Økern and Sinsen; how the thrushes ate fermented rowan berries and got drunk. I had never seen it myself, but I could picture it clearly, and I remember I wished the road to Aker Hospital would be longer than that half-hour. But it was not, and there was hardly any traffic, so it took even less time. So I stayed in the car in the car park for more than ten minutes. Several more cars arrived as I sat there, and almost everyone who got out carried flowers or nicely wrapped boxes of chocolate, and some had brought books for the people they were visiting. I hadn't brought anything.

In the end I got myself out of the car and walked towards the entrance to the surgical wards where a porter gave me directions, and then went two floors up. When I came through the glass door from the staircase and out into the corridor my father stood at the other end. I saw him at once and stopped. I don't know whether he had had the operation and was on his feet again, or if he was still waiting. I am sure he did not see me because he stood with his face to the wall, one hand above his head and the other on his stomach, and it struck me as an odd way to stand. I looked around and there was no-one else in the corridor just then. Only him at one end and me at the other, and I took a few steps towards him, and then I saw that his body was shaking, was trembling, and I went on a few more steps before I realised my father was crying. Then I stopped completely. Never once in my life had I seen him cry, and I realised from the way he was clutching his stomach that he cried because he was in pain, and he must have been in tremendous pain.

I will tell you something about my father. He was past forty when I was born, but he was different from the other men where we lived. He was an athlete. I mean a real pro. He had taken his body as far as it could go and filled it with a strength you would think it could not hold, and you could see it in the way he walked and in the way he ran, in the way he talked and in the way he laughed that there was a fire inside him that no-one could ignore, and it was clear from the way that he was *seen* that he was body and energy both, that he reached out and was heading somewhere, that there was something *about* him. And he had been that way for as long as anyone could remember. He had trained and trained to make his body into a crowbar, a vaulting pole to break free with and be lifted by. He had worn tracks into mountainsides on his way up and on his way down to strengthen his legs to get better on the football pitch, on the ski run and in the boxing ring, and on his way through town to the factory from Galgeberg and Vålerenga where he lived, and no-one *had* a strength like his. He had crossed the Østmark by every single path, up every single ridge and down on the other side, and it made him into an all-rounder. Good at everything and best at nothing. He was not fast enough. He could keep running in the tracks longer than most, but weaker men crossed the finishing line before him. He was never frontman, never anchorman, and even though no-one was untouched by his capacity for taking a beating in the ring, standing firm with his little smile, driving his opponent crazy, for much longer than anyone thought possible, it was hardly ever enough to make him one of the chosen few sent out to tournaments to fight for the club and its colours and be seen by the crowd the way he had longed for. He had the strength and he had the will, but he did not have the speed nor the imagination to give him that little extra. But that did not break him, as you might have thought. He just went on, year after year, and far beyond the point in time when what he trained for would be possible, and it made him different from all the other grown men I knew. He could endure anything. And now he stood leaning against the yellow wall of the corridor in Aker Hospital crying because he was in pain. We had not had a proper talk for as long as I could recall, maybe not since the year I was twelve and we sat by a bonfire far into the Lillomark Forest, and he showed me how a boy only 142 centimetres tall could make an asshole of 160 afraid. I suddenly felt faint and ill. There were only the two of us in that corridor, and I could not take another step. No way. I stood there for I don't know how long, and I remember thinking it was incredibly hot, that I was thirsty and wanted a drink, but I am sure he did not know I was there, for he never turned round, just held his hand to his stomach and his face to the wall as he wept, and that was what saved me. I held my breath, turned silently and walked away. Straight out of the hospital, into the car and then drove home.

I sit on the chair beside Mrs Grinde's door looking at the floor and talk and talk and do not know whether what I say and what I think are the same things, but if they are it is hard to believe, for in the years that have passed since that day at Aker Hospital I have never told anyone what happened. Not my mother while she lived, not the one who left her make-up in the bathroom, not my brother, now hovering in a stable way down in the valley between this and a different world entirely, and G. Grinde stands in front of me in the hall biting her lip and running her hand through her hair. I can't see her doing it, but I know she is, and she shifts her weight from foot to foot, not impatiently but restlessly maybe, at a loss. But when I look up she peers at me short-sightedly and says: "Are you sure he didn't know you were there?"

I look down at the floor again and say: "No."

She makes a decision then which I do not catch on to, because I am gazing down between my knees with my hands pressed to my temples, swallowing again and again and I do not see her face. It's not until much later when we lie close in the heavy warmth, and she has in fact switched the light off, that I realise it was then it happened, and yet again it strikes me what a story can accomplish.

I wake once, and it is still dark. I raise myself on my elbow and look out the window and see the light from my apartment in the opposite block, and two floors up there is light in the Hajo family home. My friend the family father stands at the centre of the room, his head bowed and his face in his hands, his whole body rocking back and forth, I can see him quite clearly, but I cannot find a way to think about it with this unknown perfume making me drowsy, and when I lie down again she turns to me under the duvet and does something that makes me gasp, it almost hurts. I cannot remember when anyone last did just that to me. And she is so warm, and her hair smells of the same perfume, it tickles my face and the way her skin touches mine makes me think of an animal whose name I do not know but would have liked to see, and once she strokes my chest and shoulders and says: "You're so fine."

"I'm like a whited sepulchre," I say. "You're the one who is fine."

She laughs then, deep down in her throat, and I laugh too although I did not mean to be funny, and she asks if I am still cold, and then I answer no, and someone says: "Do you like it when I do this?" but afterwards I do not remember which one of us it was, and then I ask: "What's your first name?" and she definitely answers something with a G, but I am already sleeping then and do not hear a thing.

6

I am flying a soundless helicopter above Oslo town. I am not yet born. That doesn't matter because I am high up and merely looking and shall not interfere. But everything is known to me. There is glass around me on all sides and a rushing silence. The city lies beneath me. It is early morning. The helicopter circles from Nydalen to the fjord, I can see the forests and the Holmenkollen ski jump and the river running through the city like a silvery-grey ribbon with all the bridges and the small boats moored to poles right down by the mouth, and nothing moves except a pale speck on its way to the river and one of the bridges crossing to the Maridalsveien on the other side. It is my father. The war is over, the party is over, spring has gone and summer has passed with its male choirs singing and laughter across the country and Norwegian flags flying from newly painted poles; the summer he rode on old buses with his white chorister's cap on his head or on the back of old lorries decorated with beech leaves and red, white and blue ribbons, the stench of bad diesel burning his nose, and he sang at the top of his voice. Now the rubbish rolls along the pavements.

Everything is black and white again, as in films. Autumn is coming, and he turns on to the bridge with the old leather briefcase under his arm, and that briefcase is so worn out that he keeps a rope tied round it to hold it together, and the late summer wind buffets his back with a hint of the first cold and it pulls at his coat, which is the same one he had ten years earlier when he bought it second-hand. It is almost white now. For five years he learned things he would never have dreamed of, and they cannot be used for anything now, cannot be told to anyone. He stops on the bridge and leans against the white-painted iron railing where the paint is peeling off in big flakes and the iron is rusty beneath. He stands there gazing into the running water until it makes him dizzy, then he has to sit down on the coarse planks with his back to the railing and his case on his lap and close his eyes. Up the road across the bridge is the factory, but he just sits there quite still as the minutes pass, seven o'clock has come and gone, and I fly around him in big circles and can see him up close and at the same time as a little white fleck, and then he straightens his back, stretches his arms out to the sides and starts breathing deeply. Slowly in and out with closed eyes, in and out with his case on his lap, in the nearly white coat and the river under the bridge and the waterfall he hears but cannot see, but which *I* can see quite clearly foaming white, and it falls and it falls, and then I start to weep so loudly it wakes me.

I am sopping wet in the face and my back is stiff. I don't know what time it is, but when I turn round it is light outside, and there's a scrap of paper on the pillow beside me. I see it at once. I run my hand over the sheet. The warmth has gone. I lie on my back looking up at the ceiling, and then I get that feeling of a film I sometimes have, though not as often as when I was younger, but sometimes, in certain situations. As if I am this man in a film and have to get inside him to play him properly and feel what he feels after a night when everything possible has happened and he wakes up in the bed of a woman he has not even talked to before, and he lies staring up at the ceiling letting everything sort of sink in, and I look at him and at the same time I *am* him. It is rather an unpleasant feeling. Because in fact it is only play-acting, and perhaps when I look up at the ceiling I do not feel anything, although *I* am the one that all this has happened to. This is what it's like, at times, but it was more frequent before, and it usually stops the minute I manage to move.

So I pick up the note and read:

"Didn't want to wake you. First to nursery school, then to work. Someone has to keep the wheels turning. There's a clean towel in the bathroom. Make sure the door locks when you leave. See you."

There is no name. I get out of bed and go out into the hall stark naked and open the door of the adjoining room. It is a child's room. A boy. I'll be damned. I must have seen them together many times, but last night I did not give it a thought. I concentrate and try to remember what he looks like, and perhaps I see the outline of a figure, a certain height, a certain width, a certain softness of the body, but I cannot see a face. I go into the living room in search of a photograph. Single mothers always have photographs of their sons on the wall. There is one above the sofa. A boy with smooth fair hair, maybe four. He is probably older now, but not much so if he goes to nursery school still. He is the boss already. He looks at me with *that* look. I am standing naked in his living room, with tears drying on my face and I am forty-three years old, and he challenges me. I lean over the sofa and turn his face to the wall.

"All right, you just glare away there," I say aloud. And then I laugh. He has been lying behind the thin wall all night hugging a teddy bear in his arms while I have had his mother in my arms and hugged her even harder, and when he was deep in a dream about a red fire engine or a spaceship with laser cannons or maybe Postman Pat with his black-and-white-cat, I was deep inside his mother both here and there and closer to her than he has been for more than four years.

"You lost," I say, "two-nil at home," and laugh again, but it does not sound too good, so I stop at once and go into the bathroom to take the shower I sorely need, and I lock the door when I leave.

*

The caretaker looks at my clothes, he is pissed off because everyone loses their keys, because he has to go out and walk several hundred metres to each block with the master key, and he is forever writing orders for new ones. He has other things to do, he says. If that is so, it has escaped me; there are light bulbs missing in most of the basement corridors, in one stairwell a pane of glass has been broken since New Year's Eve, and the mechanism of the garage door has disintegrated, and the door has been left open for two weeks. He twists the key in my lock and flings the door wide with a condescending air, and glances inside. He knows about the likes of me, he has seen pictures of me in the papers and knows what I'm up to, and he thinks it is crap. Then he gives me the slip of paper with the key number on and permission to have a new one cut.

"It will cost you," he says, "it always does when you chuck things around. Don't let it happen again. OK?"

But he doesn't hold out much hope, that's obvious, and then he goes off, on his way to his long list of chores. It is a tough life, being a caretaker.

I go in and slam the door behind me. I stand still for a moment. Then I turn and look at myself in the mirror. The swelling under my eye has quite gone and the colour is normal. My hair is still damp and has started to curl. The pale, frozen man I saw last night has vanished, you would think I lived a normal life, that I was on my way out to the bus for work after a shower. But I am not on my way to anything my father would have called a job.

The keys are on the shelf below the mirror. I cannot remember putting them there. I've never put them there before. I pick them up and stuff them in my right trouser pocket where they belong, and in the kitchen I throw the permit into the bin. Suddenly I feel so hungry it hurts. I open the fridge. There is not much left inside, and what there is I put in a paper towel and chuck out, and pour the dregs of the milk into the sink. Then I fetch a bucket, squirt detergent in and fill it with hot water, find a clean cloth in the hall cupboard, and then I wash the fridge and thoroughly dry it. After that I attack the dishes which have cluttered the worktop for ages, almost tap-dancing with impatience because I am so hungry. I wash the worktop and the kitchen table and polish the brass bowl, and I wash all the cupboard doors and the wall behind the sink and the top and the sides of the stove where I can reach, and then I stand back and study it all, and finally, not quite satisfied, I fill another bucket and wash the floor.

I change my trousers in the bedroom. I make the bed and take my dirty clothes out to be washed, then vacuum the carpet and sort the heap of books into two piles on the bedside table with Tranströmer's *Baltics* on top. "It was before the time of radio masts. / Grand-father had just become a pilot."

I must have read it ten times. It makes me think of my own grandfather who was a joiner, not a pilot, but who went down to the harbour every single day for most of his life and along the quay to look out on the sea and the changing weather towards the lighthouse far out where everything ended. He did not keep a log-book, but took careful note of ships arriving and ships departing, and at regular intervals *I* was on board one of them. He is dead now and has been for ten years, but I miss his silence and his dry wind-blown eyes and the town where he lived with him *in* it and the bottle of Aalborg aquavit he brought across the sea every Christmas. Lifeline schnapps, we called it.

While I've been doing all this I have had my pea jacket on. Now I take it off and go out on the balcony in the cold with a brush and a little cold coffee in a cup, and I brush away at the dried stains from last night, splash a little coffee on them and brush some more. It's a trick I learned from my mother, and the jacket comes perfectly clean. Not once do I look over at the window in the next block.

I switch all the lights off when I leave, feel the keys in my pocket and take the stairs two floors down to the garage under the block. For I do have a car, even though I forget sometimes. It is a thirteen-year-old white Mazda 929, a station wagon, and the first thing one of my neighbours said when I parked it in front of the block, was "Have you bought yourself an immigrant's car?"

In fact, I did buy it from a Pakistani in Tveita for 15,000 kroner, but I did not know that what I did was not quite kosher. I don't keep up with car fashions. The Mazda is really good enough, a bit rusty here and there, but it has a strong motor and holds the road well, and is as soft to drive as an American car. I haven't used it for a fortnight, so I walk round it to check whether there is a flat tyre, but everything seems fine except that someone has written "Wash me" in the dust on the bonnet. I get in and it starts at the first try as it always does, and I can drive straight out as the garage door has more or less fallen apart and stays open the whole time.

I do what the writing tells me. I drive to the Texaco station on the main road and pay fifty-five kroner for a wash with wax, buy a newspaper, then drive into position and sit in the car reading the arts section by the overhead light. That is soon done even with cheap glasses at this time of year, and the sports pages are boring now at the end of the skiing season before the football gets going. Now everyone is just waiting, and the water splashes the windows and shuts out the view, and the brushes rumble and sweep over the car, and they're green and blue and make me want to sleep, and if I wanted to sleep I could do that in a den like this, where I cannot be expected to do anything *but* wait.

But then the water stops, the brushes pull back and stop rotating, and hang there like the dead animals hunted for their fur that I've seen in Helge Ingstad's books. The door in front of me bangs open, a panel lights up over the door saying "Drive out" and I put the car into gear and it starts without problems. It is unpleasantly light outside, and I am so hungry now that my body feels numb. I had really intended to drive to a shop just a bit further away than my own Co-op to avoid the neighbours, but I cannot find one I like the look of, just drive past one place after another until I am nearly in Lillestrøm. Then I take the right turn towards Enebakk immediately before the big bridge, up the long hill through Fjerdingby, and there are several shops along the road, but I do not stop, and then there is nothing but farms and fields and forest. The road runs beside the big lake in wide curves, and sometimes you see it and sometimes you don't. Everything is in black and white like in films from the forties, the spruces are black, the snow is white and the ice still covers the lake right across to the other side where there is forest as well, and farms and grey-white fields and then forest again as far as the eye can see. This is what I like, just driving here, and it starts to snow, a few small specks at first, and then suddenly huge flakes that stick to the windscreen, and I turn the wipers on. One makes a scraping sound each time it moves to the left, but that does not matter. I turn them up to full speed and push my hand under my jacket and shirt and in to my bare chest and feel them beat in time with my heart. The snow whips against the glass and then it is swept away, hits the glass and is swept away, I drum on the gear lever and hum a tune, the whole car thumps in the same rhythm, and so does everything outside, and I feel so light, light, and I do not think of my brother or Mrs Grinde at all.

I drive through Kirkebygda where the writer Jens Bjørneboe lived and wrote *The Dream and the Wheel*, across the little river beyond the schoolhouse, past the road to the manor house where Ragnhild Jølsen of that book was born, and just after that I hit the sharp curve, and to keep up the rhythm I do not brake. This makes the car slide to the left, and as I keep a firm grip on the wheel and refuse to change course, the rear end wags and lurches, and I end up almost beam on across the road, and had there been a car coming the other way that would have meant trouble. But there isn't. I hold my breath and force the car into position, tyres screeching, and the snow turns into rain, the mercury's rising, spring must be on its way, I can feel it in my bones. Then the road straightens out along a flat stretch, and I cut the speed and lay the backs of both hands against the wheel so my fingers are free to roll a cigarette while I keep driving and peer out into the rain. The first drag tastes good, but the next one makes me feel so sick and dizzy that I stop the car at once, open the door and stagger out on to the verge, and stand there throwing up. There is not much in my stomach, but cramps take a violent hold and I stay there bent over the ditch in the rain bellowing like a cow and cannot stop.

"Holy shit," I say aloud in one of the intervals, "fucking misery." Tears pour down as I brace knees and feel the rain running down my neck. The fit finally passes, I straighten my back and see there is a house on a lawn just on the other side of the ditch. Behind it there is thick forest, almost flattened by something I could have written "was like steaming rain". On the first floor a small boy stands with his nose to the windowpane, mouth half open, staring at me with eyes almost out of his head. For a few seconds we just look at each other, he from the circle and I from the stage, and then I place my right hand on my stomach, hold the left one to the side and make a deep bow with the water streaming from my hair.

"Da capo," I mumble, stick my finger down my throat and vomit again. My stomach contracts, I cough and the pain in my side is suddenly back, oh, how welcome, old friend. My balance falters, but I jerk myself into a standing position, and now the boy in the upstairs window has both hands to his temples and his lips clenched into a line. I wipe my mouth and retreat until I feel the car against my back, raise my hand and start to wave and go on doing that until I can see he cannot help himself and waves back, and then his mother emerges from the dark room behind him. She bends forward to find out who he is waving to, and then I go around the car and get in.

When the house is out of sight I do not drive much further, just turn on to a forest track and stop a few metres along and lean back in my seat with eyes closed until my stomach feels less upset. Then I sleep for a quarter of an hour, and when I wake up I'm feeling better. It is something new in my life, this being able to fall asleep anywhere at any time. I do not know what to think about that.

I start the engine and reverse on to the road and drive through the forest and out on the other side along a field where two horses stand in the rain. One is brown, the other is black, and the sun breaks through the clouds while the rain keeps falling on the forest and the field and the farm on the hill, all seasons are queuing in the same line while everything slowly slides from grey white to dirty yellow. The two horses glitter in the slanting light as the shining rain falls mercilessly upon them, I can see each single drop as they strike like icy cold pellets and how they spurt up again, and the horses stand motionless, their heads down and their muzzles together close up to the fence, abandoned by all, being only horses with the rain coming down and down upon them, and they share no hope in this world. The sight of them totally unhinges me, I clench my jaw and I clench my fist and beat at the steering wheel, and my foot hits the gas, and all this merely because I haven't had anything to eat. But then I think: it would all be different if I had owned a horse.

There used to be a shop here I know has closed down, because I have driven this way several times, and then it has been shut. But when I come round the curve it is open, with a new sign above the door. No doubt an idealist from Oslo wants to run a country store in a godforsaken place, far from the madding crowd, but is it far enough? I don't think so. Anyway, it is open now, and I stop the car on the gravel outside, go in the door which has a sheep-bell at the top and is supposed to ring as in the good old days, and a young woman comes out of the room at the back. She smiles expectantly. No doubt, I am the first customer today, and all I want is some brown bread and a litre of milk. I put a Kvikk Lunsj chocolate bar on the counter to give my purchase more substance. She is wearing a huge apron with big stains of what looks like clay. Through the half-open door behind her I can see not an office but a pottery workshop, and when I turn round I see one end of the shop is full of bowls and vases and candlesticks and cups. All the same blue colour. I think the colour is pretty, and I think *she* is pretty. I go over, pick up a cup and weigh it in my hand, but there is no price tag on it, so I ask: "Are you expensive?"

"That one is a hundred kroner," she says, and her voice breaks slightly and she clears her throat as if it were a long time since she last spoke. It seems a lot, a hundred kroner for a cup, but then I don't know much about pottery, it may not be so costly. It is suddenly such a beautiful blue that I could not think of leaving without it.

"That's not so bad," I say, carrying the cup to the counter and putting it down in front of her. "I'll have it."

And she wraps it in tissue paper and enters the items in the till, then puts everything into a plastic bag and she looks so pretty in her apron doing this that I would not mind seeing her wearing just that apron and nothing else, and as I am thinking this she blushes. She is no mind reader so it must be the look on my face that makes her blush, and I look away, blushing myself, thinking: where on earth did that come from? But now it is there, and it may have something to do with Mrs Grinde, and then I think of her for the first time since I left her flat and how I could *feel* her and I blush again and look down at my hands as I get out my wallet and put the money on the counter. One hundred and twenty-seven kroner, ping. I would have liked to have stayed there to look at her a bit longer, watch her do things and maybe talk about pottery, but it is impossible now, and the scent of fresh brown bread seeps up from the bag and right into my face and makes my stomach feel really hollow, and I cannot very well go and buy two cups.

"Come again," she says as I am on my way out the door, and I turn in surprise and say: "Thanks."

But it is not very likely – that I will be back, or that she will be here when I do. On my way to the car I glance through the window, and she is still standing there behind the counter not looking at me or at anything at all, just straight ahead.

There is a slight breeze, but the rain has stopped. I am blinded by the low sun; it looks as if it is steaming, and the fields are steaming and the woods are, behind the shop. The gravel glitters, and when I start up there's a lump in my throat, but before I'm round the curve I tear off the first bite of bread.

7

While my father was alive I knew nothing about the photograph he had in the breast pocket of his suit the day he got married. Not until several years after his death did I hear about it from Solgunn, my aunt, on the telephone. She and Uncle Trond live in Stavanger. That is where she comes from. We have a talk from time to time. Not often, but more often than before, and it is usually one of *them* who calls. I am not so good at that, I never was.

She said: "One Christmas before you were born your mother came up to me and asked: 'How would you have liked it if the man you had been married to for two years kept a photograph of another woman in his wallet?' She used the Danish name for wallet, she was Danish, you know."

"I know she was Danish," I said, "Christ! But what did you say?"

"I answered: 'I wouldn't have liked that.'"

"Was that all?"

"What was I to say? After all, it was true. I wouldn't have liked it at all. Luckily, Trond has never done anything like that, you know."

I didn't say what I thought, that how could she know, not everyone is as clumsy as my father and drops pictures out of his wallet.

"Well," I said, "that's great for the two of you."

"I don't know what more I can say," she said, but of course she did, and we talked for quite a while.

I think of this as I drive along the gravel road from Lake Lysern and back on to the main road and over Tangen Bridge, and the road makes a bend past a shopping centre with a completely new housing area on the right, big groups of dreary houses slung up over the hillside with a view of a small lake where wooden bathing jetties are stuck in the ice along the shore.

I have had my fill now, I ate half the loaf and drank milk out of the blue cup, and I did that sitting in the car in the courtyard of my former trade union's holiday camp where I drove in just after I left the shop. I had not planned to go there, I had not planned anything, but that is where I went. From the car I could see the Lysern stretching in a narrow neck of water behind the main building, and I saw the suspension bridge crossing to the chalets on the other side. I don't know how many times I have crossed that bridge. There was ice on the water now, but the last time I was there people stood along the shore with their fishing rods and pails with perch in them, and there were rowing boats on the water and it was summer and laughter all over the place. I was going to be divorced, and I knew it. I had been waiting there a week for the woman I had seen behind me in the mirror almost every morning for fifteen years, and now I was trying to forget what she looked like. It was so hot I felt paralysed, the sun was baking, and all I wanted to do was to sit on a chair with a strong drink, but I could not do that, I had my daughters with me and had to fill the days with all kinds of things that belonged to summer so the girls would think it was a perfectly ordinary holiday. My brother had been there with his son and we had talked and talked until there was nothing more to say, until what we said grew into something that made us embarrassed, and then he had left and I was alone not knowing what to do with my days other than fill them. But on the last evening before she arrived, when the girls were in bed and I knew they were asleep, I put on the new boots I had bought because I was certain it would rain the whole week. I walked across the grass where dew had fallen and over the bridge with a wire fence along the sides which had been almost flattened by youngsters who loved to dive and jump from the edge and several metres down into the water, and on up the path I went, to the nearest chalet on the other side. The man who was staying there with his family had invited me for a drink several times, but I had refused, I could not drink, and the only thing we had in common was that we had once been members of the same union.

I knocked, someone shouted, and the boy who opened the door was in his pyjamas. He looked scared. I thought it was the sight of my face, I had not shaved or looked in a mirror for over a week and had no idea what I looked like, but over the boy's shoulder I saw his father sitting in the only easy chair the place boasted, with a glass in his hand. He called out:

"Talk of the devil, come in, come in," and it was all so stupid, I didn't even like him, and he shouted again: "Another glass, pronto."

His wife came from the kitchen and put a glass in my hand, and I went up to the chair, and he filled it to the brim with vodka. I can't take gin or vodka, but it was too late to refuse, I didn't know *what* to say, so I half emptied the glass in one big gulp, and it burned my throat and spread through my stomach like glowing lava, and I could not help coughing.

"Christ, you're not that young, you should be able to take a dram," he said, and I replied:

"Forty," when the coughing fit subsided.

"Hell, you're older than me, then. Look here," he said and filled my glass again, "try once more, and let's have a toast," and I took another swallow, and this time my stomach was prepared. But it tasted nauseous, like drinking aftershave.

"Well, sit yourself down, then," he said, but I stayed on my feet, and then he said: "Well, yes, we've seen you going to and fro, you and your chum, and we talked about it and thought for a while maybe you were gays, but then the wife said gays don't have kids, so there you are. I'm only joking, you know, so don't get mad."

"Well, we're not gay," I said, looking at his wife who was standing in the kitchen doorway, she did not want to sit down either, although there was plenty of room on the sofa and several stools. "It was my brother."

"Well, there you go. And then I had a word with one of your girls, and she said your wife is coming tomorrow, and we got the idea of the whole gang of you coming along Friday evening, and then we could have a real party, two regular families on holiday, right?"

"Ye-es, well, I don't know," I said, still standing in the middle of the floor, and he sat in the easy chair, and I knew I would never sit down in that chalet.

"I think I'd better get going again," I said, "the kids are alone."

"Shit, you can't just go off at once like that, for Christ's sake," he said, and I saw his eyes turn black and frightened like two mirrors, and he grabbed my arm and said: "Hey, don't go."

"But I really must," I said, emptying the glass. That was a mistake, for now I had downed two glasses of vodka without any water in a quarter of an hour, and there was only a scrap of chocolate and potato crisps in my stomach from an improvised feast with the girls on the last evening when everything was as it used to be, and I felt sick. I pulled my arm away and quickly made for the door.

"Just march in and drink people's booze and then bunk off again," I heard behind me, and the door slammed. I tried not to stagger, but it was not easy, it was dark now and the path was rough down to the bridge. I couldn't take vodka, and I swallowed hard to avoid throwing up. What if the girls had woken up, I couldn't go to the bathroom without hearing them call me. I walked faster and got to the bridge. Now I *had* to throw up, and I leaned on the rail, but there wasn't any rail. Jesus, I thought as I fell, this is too ridiculous. I must have made a great splash, but I did not hear a splash. I just fell and felt how cool the water was when I hit the surface, and the stillness when it closed over me, and how my boots filled up and pulled me right down as soon as I went under, and I clearly saw the newspaper headlines as I squeezed my mouth shut and tried to pull off my boots: NEWLY DIVORCED MAN DROWNS IN LAKE AT ENEBAKK, FOUR METRES FROM DRY LAND.

But someone saw me fall, and they yelled and screamed and woke the whole area and I did not drown. When I rose to the surface at last and could breathe again, I saw lights everywhere, and out of the chalets people came crowding on to the bridge, and some had torches, and two men, eager for action, played the hero, and stripped off and jumped into the water. I wanted to manage by myself and put up a fight, but they didn't back off and they pulled me ashore by my jacket collar, and there was an awful fuss, and the girls had woken up and were running in their nightdresses among the chalets searching for me, and they all thought I was pissed although I was not. Some old hags even started to mumble about child neglect, and that was how I lost my right of access to the girls when I was divorced in double-quick time a few weeks later. At first it made me furious, and then I was relieved, because I realised that if I added one thing to the other until it was all way out of control, and at the same time made myself numb and just looked straight ahead, that was a way of living that I could manage.

The traffic gets thicker. I am approaching Oslo. I drive past a sign which reads: Svartskog 3 km. Just after that I stop, signal and make a U-turn, drive back and on to the Svartskog road, up the steep hill with sharp corners I always thought looked eerie when I was small and sat right at the back of the bus looking out of the window and could not see the road at all, but only straight down into the abyss. Then I go over the top where the road levels out, and drive past Svartskog church and the big oak tree which isn't as big as I remember, but still pretty sizeable, with strong bare branches I could build houses in if I were thirty years younger or more, and then past the post office, which is still here in the middle of no man's land, and I roll down the hills alongside the forest to Bunnefjorden. At Bekkensten Quay the old kiosk has vanished without trace. No-one is fishing from the rocks now as the ice is thick along the shoreline and hundreds of metres out, and I park in the space where the kiosk used to be and walk up the hill on the gravel road with cottages on the right side of the incline to the fjord, which gets steeper and steeper as it gets to the top. The last cottage stands back from the road with a yellow-painted fence alongside the road and a yellow-painted gate hinged firmly to two posts carefully built with large stones, and in the narrow garden is a flagpole with a slack line. The cottage looks as it always looked; red-painted timbers with a slate roof, but it is so hopelessly much smaller than I remember, and it is hard to realise it can hold everything I have filled it with since I was last here in 1971. I was nineteen then. The cottage was being sold, and I had gone with my father to fetch some of his things, tools mainly and one or two chairs, and I knew he did not want to sell and had been outvoted by his brothers and sisters. They needed the money, they said. So did my father, of course, but hell, he had almost built that cottage single-handed, and even though he had good reason not to be there much any more, it was painful for him to see it go. I could understand that.

In those years my brother was at school in England, and that was why *I* went with my father to

Bunnefjorden and not *him*, and it was so unusual for one of the family to be at school in another country, in England even, that hardly anyone talked about it. I felt abandoned. I did have two other brothers, but they were younger, and I had been Little Brother for so long that it was all I was fit for, so they lived their life independently of me, and that was something my mother held against me for as long as she lived. I do not know what she thought I could have contributed.

"It's really a shame to have to sell this cottage," I said as we carried the last things out to the van we had borrowed from a neighbour in Veitvet who was a driver for a toy factory, and had his basement filled up with things he had filched from work. But he had no children.

"Do you think so?" my father said.

I said it because I knew *he* felt it was a shame and much more. To me that cottage was full of memories of uncles and aunts and bladderwrack and glass jellyfish and physical defeats I could well live without. I had no room for it. My life was filled to bursting point, and it had been like that the year before and the year before that, and as long as I had been thinking with the better part of my brain; each year bombarded me with choices I did not understand at all and which left no room for anything more; my throat was dry from running to catch up, always too late, and the last thing on my mind was fishing for mackerel and cod in the Bunnefjord. I had sweated digging trenches and laying cables for the telephone company the whole summer to make enough money to get away to visit my brother in England, and I had enough for the ticket but not for accommodation yet. I had planned to stay for four weeks, at least.

"Of course it is, isn't it?" I said.

"Sure," he said.

That was the end of that conversation. The previous day I had bawled him out and told him he belonged to the most backward part of the working class because he subscribed to *Aftenposten*, so it was not that odd that so little was said.

When we pulled the doors shut and drove down the hill towards Bekkensten Bridge I did not look back, maybe because it was I who was driving.

But my father did.

Most of the trees have vanished from the steep slope between the cottage and the water. They were felled quite recently, and still some trunks are lying in the very spot where they fell. There's a smell of fresh timber, and where the light and the view of the fjord used to be filtered through the trunks, it is open now, and bleak and miserable and drained of magic. Where before there was a little wood that held everything in place, now there is not a stone's throw to the water. Just a small quiver and it would all slide into the waves. I walk back down the hill to the car.

It is almost silly. I drive out to buy some food from a place about ten kilometres north-east of Oslo, and a few hours later I drive into town from the south, over Hauketo and up the hills near Ljan towards Nordstrand, where the East End merges into a posher West district, and though I do not have a plan it looks like a plan, for I turn into a side road among big detached houses and down past Ljan station and along yet another side road, and stop a hundred metres from the school sitting there brick-grey and massive. I glance at my watch. In ten minutes the bell will go at the end of the last lesson. I open the window and roll a cigarette, and sit and smoke while I wait. I can do it now, luckily, for this is not a good place to stand at the roadside throwing up.

I switch on the ignition and listen to the radio while I smoke and look over at the school, and when my cigarette burns down to a fag end I switch off. And then the bell goes. For just a second the sound hangs in the air, then the doors burst open and children stream out into the playground. At the gate the crowd splits up along the various roads, some go up, some down, while others stand about chatting for a bit, and a little group crosses the road towards my car. I spot the red cap at once and hear her voice through the open window. Suddenly I lose courage and sink down in the seat and stare at the dashboard. I don't even know if I am allowed to be here. But it is too late. She has seen the car and opens the door to the passenger seat, and gets in and sits looking through the windscreen. She is twelve years old.

"Hi, Dad," she says.

"Hi," I say. I pull myself up in my seat, still looking ahead. We both stare out of the window at the school.

"How are you?" she says.

"Not so bad," I say. "And you?"

"Doing fine, apart from maths."

"And your sister. Is she getting on OK?"

"She thinks everything's boring."

"That's nothing new."

She laughs. "No," she says, "but I don't know if she really means boring, even if that is what she says."

"You're probably right there."

She falls silent, then turns to look at me, I can feel it, and I can *hear* she is smiling.

"Are you going to kidnap me now, or what?"

I look at her. Her mouth is not smiling. Maybe I was wrong.

"No, well, that's not what I planned, actually," I say. As if I had been planning anything. "Would you *like* to be kidnapped, then?"

"That'd be fine, but not like in the movies, please, I have to be home by five, Mum will be back then. And I've got a lot of homework."

"An hour's kidnapping, maybe."

"That'd be great, Dad."

I haven't seen her or her sister for two months and before that only sporadically for two years. I start the car and turn by the school entrance, then drive back some distance the way I came, and out on to Gamle Mossevei beside Gjer Lake to the Villa Sandvigen, a café with a view of the water. So I have driven in a circle, for a little further on there is a signpost reading Svartskog 3 km. I park in the space facing the entrance on the opposite side of the road. When my daughter gets out and walks round the car without her rucksack on, I push my index finger into her neck, tense my thumb like the hammer on a revolver and say: "OK, hands up."

And then we march across the road. I with my finger at her neck and she with her hands in the air and a really serious face, and by the steps she says aloud: "Please, I am just a little girl. I want to go home."

"Oh yeah?" I say, just as loudly, and then I open the door. Out of the corner of my eye I can just glimpse a gaping face behind the curtain of the nearest window.

"Keep your hands up and get inside," I say.

We almost tumble over the threshold, laughing the whole way through the place and sit down at a table looking over the water. We are the only people in the café. When a man eventually comes up to the table I notice he is moving in a stiff and cautious way. I order waffles and cocoa for us both.

113

"Do you think he's called the police?" my daughter whispers before he is out in the kitchen again.

"I hope not," I say.

After a little while the man comes back with our order on a big tray he carries high above his head as if the place was crammed with people, but we are still the only ones there, and he lowers the tray in a sweeping circle and with a flourish sets white cups and plates of waffles on the table and a bowl with a silver spoon and jam. He pours the cocoa from a big white jug and when the cups are full he puts the jug down on the white cloth. He does not spill a drop. We just sit quietly watching. Everything is so white and sumptuous that half would be sufficient, and the waffles are lightly toasted and make the jam glow in the light from the window, and he makes an elegant bow and says: "Enjoy your meal," and goes off again, not stiff at all now. He can't possibly have called the police.

"Kidnapping's not half bad when you get waffles," says my daughter, impressed with the service. So am I, but I have an annoying feeling that what I have just seen is an exaggeration, a masquerade in my honour. And besides, I am chock-full of brown bread. I settle for the cocoa, take a mouthful and look out across the water.

"So you thought I was going to kidnap you," I say.

"Isn't that what divorced dads do?" she says, and it sounds like a declaration of trust I have not earned, for

I have never had a thought like that, and it's suddenly hard to sit still, hard to breathe, my legs tingle, and I get up, saying: "I just have to go to the bathroom, you eat your waffle," and then I walk between the empty tables out to the corridor and on through another room with tables as empty to the toilet at the other end. I stand in front of the basin for a bit and look at myself in the mirror. Then I turn on the cold tap and let the water run into my hands and I rinse my face and neck several times until water runs from my hair, from my nose and ears. I look round for a towel, but there isn't one, and then I have to go into a cubicle, where I pull off about ten metres of paper and use that to dry myself. Not all that successfully, and then I go back.

"Did you have a shower," my daughter says, "with your clothes on?"

"There wasn't a shower there," I say, "but it splashed out really well from the tap, so when I stood on my hands I could shower. It was a bit difficult with my jacket on, but I managed. It's important to be able to do handstands in a tight spot." She smiles, she does not believe a word I say.

"Grandfather could do handstands," she says.

She has never seen that, but I have told them about everything he did, all the things he made his body do that no-one else we knew could do.

"You eat my waffle too, I'm not really hungry."

"Then I won't have room for supper."

"Say you have a tummy ache. That will do it."

She takes the waffle from my plate and starts to eat without putting jam on, and then she quietly cries while I look out of the window and finish the cocoa, which is not that warm any longer and not quite as good as the kind I had at the hospital. On the other side of the lake a man goes down on to the ice to test it and see if it carries. He takes a few steps out and then back again. He is just a black pin figure. I turn to my daughter.

"Hi, there," I say, and she chews and chews and looks down at the table until she has finished crying, and then she wipes her face with the backs of both hands as children do and says: "Why do we hardly ever see you any more?"

I have been waiting for that question, almost looked forward to it, and still it makes me jump.

"That's not easy to explain," I say, hearing how feeble those words are, for at this moment it is suddenly *impossible* to explain. "But that's going to change," I say, and that was what I had intended to say, and I mean it, I do. She doesn't reply, just nods and goes on chewing, and I look at my watch and say: "You'd better finish your cocoa, I think the kidnapping is over for today." She gets up quickly, nearly knocking her chair over, and looks nervously at her own watch and starts to walk towards the exit. I follow her. The man who served us is in the corridor, is stiff again, and he barely nods and does not say "Come again". I feel his eyes on my back across the road to the car park where my car stands all by itself looking vulnerable in a way I cannot explain, and it makes me annoyed. I force myself to stop and take a long look around before I unlock the car door. I look back at the café as firmly as I can, and then I look over Gjer Lake. It has been quite a day. There has been snow, there has been rain, and after some time there was sunshine, and now the fog comes stealing over the ice like milky-white soup, it oozes up the shores and rises to roll across the road and hides the signpost with directions to Svartskog. Before we have settled into the car the fog has reached us, and it swells past the windows and wraps us up. We close the doors and I start the engine and drive carefully the whole way alongside the lake and cross back to the fjord again, then up among the houses in Herregårdsveien and past the school. I stop beside the little skating rink on the bend just before the house where she lives; around it the big properties are studded on the slope behind the shining ice, greyish white with the fog that welds them together, some of them old and dignified, some new-rich and ugly-looking. We sit in the car watching the world disappear.

"Do you still have to sleep with the light shining in your face?" I ask.

"No, I've grown out of that."

"That's good," I say, but I do not mean it, because even though it may sound silly I do not want her to grow out of anything that I cannot see, I want her to wait for me. But I can't very well tell her that.

She opens the door quietly, picks up her rucksack and stands with a hand on the door for a moment before saying: "Do I have to tell Mum about this?"

"I don't really know, it's probably best not to."

"Fine," she says, "see you," she says, looking as if she is about to lean into the car towards me, but she changes her mind, shuts the door and starts to walk with the pack on her back up the gravel road to the tall yellow Swiss chalet where they live on the first floor. Maybe with some other man. I do not know. I did not ask.

8

I drive through the fog over Lambertseter and on to the ring road for E6 and head north. Everything moves in slow motion, the rear lights of the car in front are the only things I see, no sudden movements, no loud sounds, nothing but this milky-white soup in which everything flows silently as in a sleepwalker's dream. I feel tired again, I want to go to sleep. I calculate distance with speed to find out how long it will take me to get home, and I realise I am in for trouble on the way. It's rush hour, the car in front moves slower and slower until it almost stops, and I have to squeeze my eyes to focus enough not to drive into it from behind. I keep blinking and count the books I have read, take each author in turn and start with the ones I like best. A line of cars steals slowly past me on my left like the shadow of a ship, it is tall and mysterious, it is *Pequod*, it is the barque *Zuidersee*, it is the *Flying Dutchman*, hardly a light to be seen, but not like in Wagner, for everything is a quiet murmur and feels almost safe, and darkness sinks inside the car. I am nodding off, there is a rushing in the treetops, I am skiing through Lillomarka with my father, but I do not want to, my body is not like his body, I am only twelve and I am worn out, and he wants to go on and on, and he coaxes me, he tempts me on, and then insults me, and he does not stop. The snow is wet, grey and slushy, it slides from the trees around me and hits the ground with a sticky plop. Everywhere there is dampness in the air, as in the baths I hate, and I do not recognise the places we pass and I am afraid he will leave me. At the same time I want him to. Leave me. Everything is floating in this fog, and I do not notice my car veering across to the next lane before metal scrapes metal. The driver in the big van beside me sounds his horn and wakes me up with loud hooting and banging on his window. I jump in my seat and turn my car back into my lane and put on speed as I feel a banging at my rear bumper and then a second driver leans on his horn. I should have stopped now to see if there was any damage, but it's not possible, there are thousands of us gliding the same way in a slow stream, and I open my eyes wide and look for a way out. I glimpse an opening to the right, signal and move across. I barely make it. There is hooting all around me. It is the grand finale. I cross again and get into the bus lane. Now I can go no further. The next lane is solid rock. I stare through the windscreen watching for the first turn-off. Yellow and black, yellow and black, it's almost impossible to see, but then there is suddenly yellow and black. I am in the right position and sail up the slip road looking in the mirror to see if there is anyone on my tail. There isn't.

There is a roundabout at the top. If I cross straight over it is sure to lead down on to the motorway again, so I turn to the right past a bus stop and on beside some garages by a housing block, and stop in the shelter of the far wall. I don't know where I am, but that does not matter. I have the garage wall on one side and a container on the other. It feels suitably safe. It is warm in the car. I switch off the ignition and close my eyes, and there is mist everywhere. Mist everywhere and my father's broad back and big lumps under my skis. It is like walking on snowshoes. Helge Ingstad wore snowshoes in the forests of Canada, but he had a dog team, and a sledge and beaver skins and he smoked a pipe in the pictures from the book *A Fur Trapper's Life*. I have Splitkein skis and Kandahar bindings. Kandahar is a town in Afghanistan. Where Splitkein is, I do not know. Maybe nowhere. I raise my ski pole and lay it against my cheek like a gun with the ring at the end as a sight and let it slide round me and I *see* it all: tree behind tree behind tree and the track like a ribbon of shadow into the grey. Suddenly the snow on the nearest spruce breaks loose, slides down through the branches and plops on to the ground. I whip round and take aim, a squirrel in its greyish-brown fur streaks up the trunk and I fire before it reaches the top. A cone comes falling, yellow and heavy, and it sinks into the snow and vanishes, and I whisper: I could never kill anything.

But I can think about it. I could go hunting in the deep forest all winter long, inspect the traps at regular intervals and make friends with the Indians, count the furs in the spring, load up the sleigh in late March and dash off with well-rested dogs down to the Hudson Bay Company and get money in the bank.

He is far ahead on the track and he is calling me and wants to go on, but he is not really *going* anywhere. He gets up at five every morning, and sits alone in the kitchen having his breakfast while I lie upstairs awake and listening to the silence filling each cubic metre of air all the way upstairs, and he is not even listening to the radio. Then he fills his lunch box and leaves with a click of the door, and he is not going anywhere. He just goes on.

But you could say no. You could just leave everything and choose a different road.

"Come on," he calls, "we'll take a short cut." He points with his pole in the direction of the track and makes two vigorous sweeps. "Watch out, it's a steep slope here," and he starts off downhill, knees bent low and his poles straight out from his armpits like two wings. I go over to the top where he stood before and watch him sail down the long hill like a great, blue-white bird, on his way going nowhere. I turn and see the main track we have left far away between two summits, it makes a bend into the forest, and there are people there, although I cannot hear their voices.

When I look back my father has vanished. There are only the pine tree trunks and the long white hill and the misty air, and I do not know where I am and cannot turn back. I push off with my poles and almost sit right down on the heels of my boots and glide off. The track takes a long turn, and when I come round it a warm wind rises along the ridge. It's a wicked wind, and the going is so slow that I stand up again and I see the white surface of a lake down below, and just by the lake behind a tree there's a dark shadow. A dead animal, I think, a roe deer, but it is no animal. It is my father in the deep snow, his face resting against one shoulder and his poles straight out. I stop before reaching him. Something is wrong. His face is white and he moves his jaws as if chewing, there is gravel in his mouth and it crunches when he says: "Is that you, Arvid."

"Yes."

"Can you take my skis off?"

I do not want to, but I must. I take off my own skis and walk round him in the snow. Then I see his foot. It is sticking out the wrong way and isn't like anything I have ever seen before. I bend down and pull hard on the buckle and he groans aloud. I stand up quickly and say:

"Shit, don't do that," and my father turns his face even closer to his shoulder, and in the white snow he seems a lot smaller. I bend down and pull again. His foot slides out, looking weird, and then I unfasten the other ski.

"Come here," he says. His voice is stronger now. I take two steps and stand close to him, and he takes a hold round my hips and starts to hoist himself slowly up.

"Now you just stay there," he says, and his body grows big again, and heavy and about to drag me down through the snow and deep into the ground. I plant my feet firmly and look another way, look out on the water where the ski track crosses to the other shore. No-one has been on it for a long time, the snow looks wet and hellish, and there is open water in two places.

He is standing up now, he leans on my shoulder, his knees are shaking, and he looks in the same direction as I do, saying: "I didn't see it before it was too late, I just threw myself to the side, there was no time to turn." And then there's a scraping sound. Shivers run down my back as I realise my father is standing close to my ear grinding his teeth. I twist aside, and he starts to slide.

"Fucking hell," he says, and his hands scrape over my sweater, over the zigzag pattern and down my stomach, he is pulling me with him, it is an avalanche with us both right inside the fall, and we land in the snow with him on top. I hit out and kick to free myself, his wet anorak against my face, I cannot breathe, it's like drowning, I get frightened and scream:

"Let go of me," and roll aside and get to my knees and then all the way up and I stand and breathe as best

I can while my father groans again, clenches his teeth and lifts the damaged leg with both hands out from under his body. His forehead is wet and he looks at me as if I wasn't his son at all and says: "It's no good, Arvid. You must go for help."

I look up the long hill. I could never do that, neither with nor without skis.

"You can go across to the main track," he says, "there are people there." He indicates the direction I must take and I look that way, but I don't give a damn about people.

"I don't want to," I say, and I mean it.

"You must, I'm afraid," my father says. That is not true, he is afraid of nothing, but he is right, I have to go. And anyway I don't want to stay. I don't want to go, and I cannot stay, so I just start to walk, without my skis, into the forest with the wet snow up to my ankles, and only once do I turn and see him sitting with his head against a tree, gazing into the air with his pale dripping wet forehead and his patriot's hairstyle.

"You'll be fine," he says aloud, "you can do it," and I can only just hear him and I feel the weight of his head right over to where I am standing, but he does not turn, and it does not matter what he says, because everything closes off behind me and I am alone.

I walk. Snow begins to fall, wet flakes down my neck, and I don't know what time of day it is, and I am hungry, and maybe it will soon be evening and

125

darkness will fall. I choose a tree far ahead and walk until I reach it, and then choose a new one and tell myself I can rest when that is behind me. But I do not stop, just pick out more trees until I cannot go on any further and sit down on a stump. The stump is next to a spruce with its branches weighed all the way down by snow to form a shelter only I can know. No-one can see me, all around is silence. Straight in front of me there is a round clearing all covered with snow. I lean against the trunk and look up through the branches thinking there might be a squirrel at the top. I don't know how long I sit there. When I stand up and look out on the clearing I see a shadow first and then a huge elk moves alongside the trees opposite me. Its long legs move cautiously and it does not like the going, its whole body quivers nervously, and each time a hoof sinks into the snow it quickly comes up as if it was a dance. I feel the mild wind in my face and know I am well placed. It is my first elk, but I know it from the books of Mikkjel Fønhus, it is misshapen and beautiful, and heavy and light both, as it dances across the clearing like a creature from some other world and it will soon vanish among the trees on the opposite side. Calmly, I raise my hands and grip a gun I do not have, close one eye tight and aim with the other, and shout: "Bang."

The elk jumps and turns at the same moment. The great body hauls itself forward, but it does not get anywhere, for something holds it back, and it falls on its side in the snow. I look down at my hands, what has happened to them, what have they done; I didn't mean any harm, didn't mean any harm, I rush from my shelter and out into the clearing, yelling:

"I meant no harm," and then the elk kicks the empty air, whipping slush from its hooves in lofty curves and gets up in a way I will never forget, like a fall in a film in reverse, coming up and up in a snowy cascade, trembling and struggling to be standing again before trotting on across the clearing, into the shadows and is gone.

I run on and pass the big hollow in the snow where the elk fell and I feel sick. But I control myself and just run on as if running is the only thing in the world I want to do, and I run across the clearing and in among the trees and do not stop until I get to a slope, and there I put on new speed and sail over the edge and slide on my slippery ski boots all the way down, and when I stop at the bottom I am standing in the middle of the main ski track. The lamps are out, so it must be daytime still.

But where is everyone? I look up to the nearest bend. All is quiet that way and downhill it is quiet, nothing but my own breath and the misty air, and I do not know which way leads where. I close my eyes and stand completely still and imagine I can lift myself out of this forest, float away and be suddenly grown up, and look back at this with time in between, or *not* look back and forget it all. And then the silence suddenly whirls away. There is the noise of dogs and voices, two teams come down the track from the hill above, the men shouting strange words, and the dogs reply. I place myself in the middle of the track with my arms out to both sides. They brake and the men shout again and then they come to a stop. I look at them and they look at me and the dogs are panting. The nearest one has eyes that are completely yellow, and a smell comes from the dogs' bodies that has nothing to do with my life, and I like that.

The tallest man walks round the sledge, stops in front of me and says: "Are you standing here waiting for a bus?" He smiles, but there is nothing I can say to that. I keep my arms stretched out.

"Where are your skis?" he asks.

I point into the forest.

"Has something happened?"

"I shot an elk," I say. The man starts to laugh, then he turns to his companion and says:

"Did you hear that? He's shot an elk. Not bad, not bad at all." He looks at me again.

"What with, if I may ask?"

I show him my hands, and my face and neck start to tingle, and then my neck and then my fingertips.

"That's not what I meant to say. It's my father."

"You have shot your father?"

I look at him. "I don't know," I say, and then I hear

a rattling sound. It fills my head. It hurts. The man in front of me thrusts his hand into his anorak pocket and pulls out a chocolate bar, unwraps it and pushes it between my teeth. I bite it right off. And the odd thing is I don't remember anything after that. Not a thing.

Somebody is knocking at the windscreen of my car. I roll the window down. He puts a hand on the roof and almost leans inside.

"You can't stay here," he says. "Didn't you see the sign?"

He is wearing overalls. There is something familiar about the way he leans against the car. He must be a caretaker. There is a notice on the garage wall: No Parking. Vehicles left here will be toed away at owner's cost. I had not seen it.

"There is a 'w' in 'towed'," I say.

"What?"

"There's a 'w' in 'towed'. It is spelled 't-o-w'. Can I sit in the car while they tow it?" I ask. He doesn't answer that, so I ask: "Where will I be towed to, then?"

"Ullevål. It will cost you. It doesn't pay to get lost."

"I know," I say, "I have heard that one before. Thanks for the offer, but that would be the wrong direction." I start the car, saying: "And thanks for the chat. I feel much better now."

I roll the window up, he takes his hand off the roof and I back out and turn the car, drive past the garages and out on to the road back to the roundabout by the E6. He stays in the mirror in his overalls, hands on hips and head to one side, and I look around and see housing blocks everywhere. The fog has lifted, it is Furuset. I am in Furuset. Then I can take the Gamle Strømsvei across Lørenskog and on home.

I drive along Strømsvei with a wall of rock on the right and the motorway straight down on the left and over a bridge to the other side past the big Publishers' Centre warehouse where I am sure I haven't got a book left, every unsold copy shredded, and on to Karihaugen where a woman was murdered twenty years ago, driven away and buried under the snow in Nittedal. Her name was Berit and her husband was in the editorial office of *Dagbladet*, weeping because he missed her so and wanted to help *Dagbladet* with their daily reports on the investigation, and then of course he was the one who had done it. "I am Berit. I have gone away," the poet Jan Erik Vold chanted on his record of that year with Jan Garbarek on saxophone, and Dag Solstad wrote a novel a few years later. I still remember her picture in the paper. It was the first tabloid murder in Norway, and I think of it every time I drive past.

I stop at the optician's in Lørenskog where I am pretty certain I have phoned and ordered new glasses. Tentatively, with an innocent smile, I ask if I can collect them now, in case I *did* call, playing the distrait professor who forgets most things in everyday life and everybody knows he cannot be any different. The lady behind the counter laughs and joins in the joke and pulls out the drawer with completed orders in little brown bags and leafs through them, and there they are. I throw out my arms and laugh too, for after all it was just a joke, and of course I did remember. But it will cost you when you lose things. Maybe more than I have got. I swallow and use my Visa card and hope for the best. I need those glasses. I want to work, and I can't do that without them.

"Approved" comes up on the screen after a pause. I get a receipt I can use against tax and push the case with my new glasses deep down into my pocket. I leave and get into the car and drive to Skårer and out on to Gamleveien, over the open country and up past the church and the school on the hill and on past farmland towards the ridge until I turn off the road up the bend to the hospital. The helicopter is on its pad with its insect wings at rest. It seems a long time since last I was here, but it is less than twenty-four hours.

It is daylight now. I thought it was easier last night. And then I think about that night and the cocoa I had that tasted so mysteriously good and of the time when my brother and I came home from Denmark six years ago in a borrowed van we had far from emptied, and it was still a spring of some kind, the longest ever. He went off to his life, and I went off to mine, and then silence fell. I do not know what happened. I do not know what *didn't* happen. We had a mission. We had to empty the flat we had grown up in and sell to the highest bidder as quickly as possible. It would actually take us a year to finish that job, but we did not know that then. He would call me early to say he was on the way from his home at Fetsund and coming round, for I had no car then, and after twenty minutes he bowled up in front of the block and we drove down to Oslo and the suburb of Veitvet. We stayed there for an hour or less, picked things up and put them down again, went down to the basement to fetch tools, filled a cardboard box or maybe two and sat on the sofa going through old papers or old photographs of the cottage at Bunnefjorden from the time my father built it almost single-handedly, looking like Johnny Weissmuller or a sculpture from ancient Greece. Like the guy with the discus. And then we gave up and locked the door and stood by the hedge in front of the terraced house talking with a neighbour we had always known, and he wondered how we were getting on. We had no idea how we were getting on. We did not fly any more, we did not float any more. We were on our way to the bottom, but we did not see that. And then we went home. We used to stop at Gjeller Hill, on the way out of Oslo, at Morten's Inn, and we had dinner there and glanced sideways at each other and looked out of the window and did not utter one sensible word. It was like walking through syrup. On the way out to the car my brother always went ahead of me, and he could look so heavy and exhausted, and he stared at the ground as if each thought was a torture, and it made me so annoyed it almost frightened me.

9

I go through the doors and sit down in the arrival hall or vestibule or foyer or whatever it is called, where everyone passes on their way in or out and waits for the lift or buys the flowers they have forgotten, or sweets, or lousy novels in paperback editions because they do not remember the rules for hospital behaviour until they have them pointed out right here, or just sit waiting in dread on a chair with a coffee or a Coke on the table in front of them to stretch the time.

The coffee tastes horrible. And I cannot smoke. I look around me. There is a dividing line here, I know it, a before and an after, in this very vestibule or foyer, and I know exactly where. It is over there by the lift. I can stride over and with a piece of chalk show where the line will go on the floor, if anyone is interested, and I do not talk about much margin of error, a couple of centimetres at the most, and in a whole life that is not a lot. After all, I am forty-three. After all, I have seen plenty. In real life. On video. An elk falling dead and getting up again. A woolly penguin on a bunk. Water closing over and then falling silent. My father on the floor in a sea of beer, or was it blood, skin to skin with other bodies. Suddenly I do not remember clearly, but I *know* I have seen it.

I push away my coffee cup, stand up and go out the way I came in and stand to the right of the entrance smoking a cigarette just beside a huge concrete ashtray. I am not alone. A man in a wheelchair beside me nervously sucks his cigarette. He looks worn out. I don't want to think about what is wrong with him. Behind him a nurse in green stands gazing into the air at nothing.

I look over at the helicopter still standing quietly on its pad with its rotor blades hanging, being nothing now but several tons of dead metal, and I look at the car park where my car stands among hundreds of others. It has got a small dent in the back bumper and a nasty scrape along the front left wing. Maybe I can get one second-hand. Maybe I should look for a job. I have hardly any money left. I don't know. Above all, I must sleep, and then I must think of something.

I finish my cigarette, bend down and stub it out in the big ashtray which is full to the top and would make almost anyone stop smoking. I feel a slight pain in my side when I straighten up. Automatically, I lift my hand and press it against the bottom rib and what I fear is something new and unknown a little further in. The nurse turns and looks at me, and even though his face is quite expressionless I suspect a certain irony and think: he knows something I do not know, and I let my hand fall. I avoid his eyes and look past him at the emergency entrance a bit further on where an ambulance approaches, turns and stops with its back to the entrance. The driver gets out and walks round the vehicle to open the back doors, and two nurses come out of the hospital; a man and a woman. He is tall and strong, she has rather severe-looking glasses. They pull the stretcher from the ambulance and snap down the wheels, straighten some tubes hanging from a pole, I can see blood all the way from where I stand, and for just a second *she* looks over at me and stiffens. It is Mrs Grinde in a green nurse's uniform. And then she looks at her watch. I don't know why, but she glances down at her watch and looks over at me again, and then I do the same thing. I look at my watch. It is half past four. That tells me nothing except the time of day. When I look up again they are on their way in with the stretcher between them. I walk quickly over there, past the ambulance and over to the glass doors and stop outside, and stay there staring in. I am not allowed to go in there, but I see Mrs Grinde's back by the stretcher moving at full speed and the tall man on the other side. Someone comes running and puts something into her hand. I can't see what it is, but they do not stop, she just half turns and takes it as they hurry on. Her body is indecipherable in the shapeless green uniform and might look like anything at all, but it does not, she has a quite specific shape, a quite specific curving and extension and warmth, and if I have not thought about her once today that I can recall now, I can *feel* her all the same, as a half-blind animal does underground when it turns in deep darkness beside another, and nothing but that movement is important, and then the next, until skin and skin become one skin; no glasses, because no-one need see anything anyway, no green uniform or brothers with tubes down their throats or roaring helicopters or Zen Buddhist manoeuvres on cold nights.

But why did she look at her watch?

I go back to the main entrance and walk in, cross the wide hall past the Narvesen kiosk and cafeteria tables on the left where my coffee cup waits on one of them half full and abandoned, and right over to the lifts. I press the bell and wait. There is a ping and when the doors open I cross the line.

I leave the lift and walk down the corridor to the intensive care room and push the door open. A little too hard, maybe, I didn't mean to. The man in the bed there is quite unknown to me. He is not my brother, anyway. He is wounded in the face and his head is bandaged, as are several places on his body, and there is plaster on both legs and a collar round his neck. His head is clamped in a kind of steel device screwed together on both sides, and only his eyes move. They grow big and frightened and stare at me as I burst in. I stop in the middle of the floor and the door shuts behind me with far too loud a sound, and I say:

"I'm sorry, I took the wrong door. I will go again. Oh, shit." This last is to myself mostly, and I back towards the door. He moves his lips. He wants to say something. I stop and go back to the bed and bend over him. His breath is faint on my face.

"What?" I say.

"Please," he whispers. His eyes fill with tears, they run over in a rush and roll down his face that gets soaking wet, wounds and all, I have never seen such a flood, and he whispers: "Please, please."

"But for God's sake, I am not going to hurt you," I say, whispering too. I feel I'm getting really annoyed, this situation is meaningless. I straighten up and walk over to the door again.

"I will fetch someone," I say over my shoulder on the way out.

I stand in the corridor with my back to the wall. It's as if I had been running. I am breathless. And then I go to the nurses' office. I knock on the door frame and put my head through the open door. It is the same nurse as last night.

"Hi," I say.

She turns and recognises me. Reports or notes or whatever they are called are on the desk, and to the right is the jug of cocoa. That much cocoa can't be good for you. She puts her pen down.

"Your brother has been moved to the next floor down," she says. "He is conscious now. How are you doing? Did you get a good night's sleep?"

"Couldn't have been better. I slept like a baby. But the man in intensive care doesn't feel so good."

"We know. That is why he is there."

"I think he wants to talk to someone."

"He mustn't talk. He must have complete rest. It is important."

"OK," I say, "that's settled, then. You're the boss. I had better slip down a floor then."

"Yes, you do that."

She turns to the desk and her journals again and picks up her pen. I should have said something about stability, I guess, but nothing comes to mind.

I do not use the lift, but take the stairs down the one floor and go from the landing in through the glass doors to the ward. His bed is in the corridor. It is too sudden, I have no time to prepare myself, there is nowhere to hide and I cannot turn because he is not lying down, he is sitting up in bed waving his arms and laughing. His wife Randi is sitting on a chair by the bed. She catches sight of me and waves. I have not seen him this lively for ages. I walk up to them slowly, breathing as deeply as I can and letting the air slowly out, and I fetch a chair and sit down beside Randi. She looks at me, shrugs slightly, and does not seem to be having any fun at all.

"There you are at last," he says, "come to visit your brother. So now there is no-one else, is there? Now we are a plenary session." He laughs loudly.

"I was here last night," I say.

"You were?"

"Yes."

He falls silent, he leans against the wall and smiles, but he is not smiling at me or at anyone else that I can see, and then he laughs again and says: "I was just telling Randi about the time you and I went up to Aluns Lake to fish in the drinking water even though it was strictly forbidden, and we met the tramp who had moved into the forest to avoid all the shops that sold beer and all the wine monopolies so he couldn't get drunk, and now in the evenings he just sat looking at the lake, scouting for beavers, and lived on canned food, and how he helped us reel in the big pike we took home with us later and did not dare show anyone because we had broken the law, and then we put it in the basement store, and there it lay until it went completely rotten and started to stink like hell."

He takes a breath and goes on, and the thing is that nothing he says is true. It is something I once wrote in a novel mixed up with a story by Raymond Carver I know he has read, because I asked him to and we talked about it afterwards. It is only a year or two ago.

"Do you remember the smell of him?" my brother says. "Of bonfire and pine needles and marshes, and how we loved that smell, and how we wanted to live a life like his, but we were too young, weren't we, and we had to go to school, and how that made us furious." He smiles, what he says is just crap, and I cannot understand why he talks like this, for we never have shared such an experience, never shared those words, but *I* can clearly remember thinking like this when I was a teenager and have often done so since, and I never heard my brother say he had the same ideas. It was *my* secret, all that, and no-one knew a thing about it until I started to write about it many years later.

Randi bites her lip and looks at me to find out what to think about this stream of words, but I cannot help her and in fact do not want to, and then she steals a glance at her watch and says: "David has already been at home on his own for two hours, I'd better be going."

David is their son, he is the same age as my older daughter, barring three days. When my brother hears his name he blinks several times and his face goes stiff. Randi does not see that, she bends down and gives him a quick hug. Then she stands up, and he is just as stiff.

"Take care," she says, "see you tomorrow," and walks down the corridor to the glass doors, and she is a stylish lady seen from behind, with brisk, determined steps on her way away from this place and maybe much further, maybe to a whole new life, and I stay on alone beside the bed with the vacant chair at my side. My brother stares at that chair.

"I am so tired," he says, not raising his eyes. He lies down and pulls the duvet up to his chin, closes his eyes and opens them again and looks up at the ceiling, and

I think of how I would like to know what he sees up there, and then I realise that it is not true. It is just something people say when they do not know what else to say.

People are walking along the corridor behind me, it is visiting time for others as well, and they laugh and talk loudly, and I turn and see they are correctly dressed in newly pressed civilian clothes, bringing flowers and chocolates, and even lousy novels in paperback editions under their arms. I stay twisted round in my chair staring after them, and I do not want to turn back. I have nothing to say. And then I say:

"So you thought you could just go off and leave me on my own, did you?"

The chocolates people are talking at the end of the corridor. Someone opens a door to another room and closes it again. There is someone crying in that room. Otherwise all is quiet. Maybe my brother has gone to sleep. I hope so. I look at him.

"You won't do," he says. His voice is completely empty, there is nothing there for me.

"OK," I say.

"I want to sleep," he says, turning his face to the wall.

"That's OK."

I sit on the chair looking at his back and the back of his head with the curly hair growing thinner. He has a bald patch now. I do not recall seeing that before.

"OK. So long," I say.

"So long," he says to the wall.

I get up and go. At the end of the corridor I stop and look back. A nurse comes along pushing a screen which she arranges in front of his bed.

I do not wait for the lift, but make for the stairs, and there are many floors, six or seven, or maybe eight, I seem to lose count, and I more or less run the whole way down, and it's like sinking, and there is hardly anyone on those stairs. Only once there are two men coming slowly up, side by side, step by step, and they talk and look at each other, and I do not want to go round them, to change direction, it is too much trouble, so I aim right between them. There is really not enough room, so I snarl:

"Out of the fucking way," and push the one to the left in the shoulder. He curses and I hear them stop and feel them staring at my back. But *I* do not stop.

On the ground floor, I stop running, but I still walk quickly, I can out-walk most people if I decide to, and through the big hall I slacken speed so much it almost looks normal. It is crowded with people and all the tables are taken. That is all right by me. I am on my way out.

It is raining in front of the hospital. The helicopter has gone. I run again, across the tarmac in the rain to the car park, and suddenly I forget where I left my car.

I run up and down the rows. There are many more than when I arrived, several rows of brand new cars. How people can afford such new cars is more than I can grasp, fuck it all, I shout, fuck it all, where the fuck is my old car, and the rain pours down as if possessed, and it cannot go on like this. I can't take it any more. I must get away, I must go somewhere new, see completely different things than this misery here, see some other country with different people. And then there it is, my white Mazda with a handsome scrape on the left front wing. I unlock the door and get in, hair and shoulders sopping wet, and picture sea voyages when boats were boats and not floating casinos, and they rolled with the waves as they were meant to do, with wind sweeping the decks, and all the places I would dream about were far, far away.

10

I was nineteen and came down to Gothenburg late at night from off the Europa road, and it was late September and the sky was dark above the big town. The lorry driver had shown me which way I should go and which sign to look for to get out along the lighted streets to the harbour area at the other end and further on all the way to where the boat for England was moored, and it was a long stretch, he said, and it certainly would be dark there and quite deserted, but I liked the walking, I had plenty of time, my boat did not leave until next morning. I had taken no chances and would not miss it. Now I had a night before me.

I had been up at dawn that morning to avoid disturbing my parents, and everything went well and quietly until I had to go into the living room to fetch something I had forgotten, and then my youngest brother sat on the stairs. He was seven years old and had very shiny, almost white hair, and he sat there in his pyjamas full of warm sleep, looking at me and waiting, and saying nothing. I really did not know him very well, I was twelve when he was born and had bought my first record player, and after that my eyes were looking in quite other directions than to the living room at home, but he was a good lad, and we were always very polite to each other. Now I went up and sat down on the same step.

"You're awake early," I said.

He nodded.

"I am going away now," I said, "to England. I shall be away for quite a long time."

"I know," he said, and then he was quiet, and then he said:

"Is it true that the Beatles aren't together any more?"

"I'm afraid it is."

"You won't meet them, then."

He had heard that music since the cradle. It had always been there, on the radio and the record player, and now it was over, and that took a long time to sink in.

"Maybe I shall meet them separately. If I see Paul McCartney I will send him your love," I said, and then he smiled. We had discussed it several times; he liked McCartney best, and I liked John Lennon, but I felt generous that morning and several good songs came to mind that McCartney had written.

"That's great." He stood up and said: "Have a good time, then," and shook my hand in a solemn manner.

"You have a good time too," I said, and gave his hand a little squeeze, and he went up to bed again, and

I took the tube into Oslo and walked along past Østbanestasjonen and the railway line to Mosseveien, and there I took my place by a petrol station with my thumb out. There had been rain in the night, but now the sun was bright and there was a sharpness in the air that felt good and a sparkle on the fjord that I knew so well, but it had already turned into something different, and the town behind me seemed changed, and the Ekeberg ridge and the merchant navy college like a fortress up there, and the pale blue tram on its way to the top had also changed.

I was wearing the old pea jacket I thought was like the one Martin Eden wore when he went ashore at San Francisco in Jack London's best novel and was about to haul himself up by the hair into a new life of knowledge. That was what I wanted too. The jacket must have been ten years old, and I had bought it from the Salvation Army, and even if I could not remember if Martin Eden *really* had a pea jacket in the book, he should have done, and I was fond of that jacket, I had used it almost every day for more than a year. I had pinned an FNL badge to the collar, and in my backpack I had a warm sleeping bag and a watertight notecase and three books to keep me linked to the world; Bobby Seale's *Seize the Time*, about the Black Panthers; Svend Lindqvist's *The Myth of Wu Tao-tzu*, the one that ends with the question: Is social and economic liberation possible without violence? No. Is it possible *with* violence? No. And I had Paal-Helge Haugen's *Leaves from an Eastern Garden: 100 Haiku*. They were good to read early in the morning.

I was leaving my childhood behind and my father and all he stood for and all he was not, and it had taken its time, but I felt fearless now standing at the edge of the road and free to choose my own life, full of love for the future, and only fifteen minutes later a trailer truck came panting out by Loenga and stopped a little way further along the road. The driver softly sounded his horn as a signal to me to join him.

Now I was walking in a Swedish night, with an all-Norwegian pack on my back on my way through a town where the sea air blew in quite differently from the fjord at home, and the houses were not unlike those I was used to seeing, but still somehow different; somewhat higher and somewhat more beautiful, and all crafted with some other stone containing some other glow that I did not know, and canals traversed the town reflecting the street lights, and they were yellow and orange and almost red in the oily water, and there was music from an open window. It was something from an opera, and I had never liked opera, but I did like opera now, and I remember singing, but I do not remember which song.

The truck driver was right. It was a long way. I had to walk right through the town in a semicircle around the harbour area and past the shipyards that had not yet closed down, and on northwards almost right out to Torslanda airport and the Volvo factory, and I walked and walked, and when I got there the night was far advanced and there were no street lamps, only one or two chance lights and some lamps by the ferry quay where I could feel the sea like a sigh, but I could not see it.

There was an oil refinery there with BP painted in yellow and green on the great shiny tanks and a tower where a gas flame crackled and burned at the top and threw enough light for me to find my way up between two big rocks. I decided it would not rain that night and unpacked my sleeping bag and spread it straight on to the ground and crept into it with all my clothes on. I was exhausted and happy and fell asleep at once, and the few times I woke I looked straight up at the sky with its multitude of stars, and I knew the names of the biggest ones, and I saw the gas flame shining and heard it crackling and felt at home in the world.

What finally woke me was the sound of steps and the sound of bicycle wheels and the squeaking sound of pedals on chain guards and a bus stopping and opening its doors. I heard voices and someone laughing, and I sat up in my sleeping bag, rubbed my eyes and peered over the top of the rough grey knoll in front of me. Everything was completely clear. I saw the sea straight out and bare sloping rocks and low islands in the light of a low sun, and at the quay lay a large boat with the name *M/s Spero* painted on its side. The British ensign aft waved gently in the light wind, and it was a warm morning for September. Between the rise where I was lying and the quay there was a road which was the same one I came along last night, and now a stream of people in blue were making their way from the south part of town to where the Volvo factory was situated with its great gates and its logo in a circle above them. It was clear to see at the end of the road. One man turned and looked at my head sticking up, and even at a distance he was obviously smiling, and then I raised my hand and waved, and he waved back, and then several men turned, perhaps ten or twenty of them, and they all smiled and raised their hands and waved.

By the time the ferry had sailed I had read two haiku by Basho about the vast night falling on a road where nobody walks, and packed the book tidily in my rucksack again.

The sea was quiet and calm off the coast of Sweden and a little boring across the Kattegat until we rounded the completely flat tip of Denmark at Skagen, and then we were in the North Sea with a wind sweeping the deck, and the boat rolling as it was meant to roll, and at breakfast time the cups flew off the table and hit the floor with a loud clatter, and some of them broke, and no-one managed to get a mouthful in before the third try. Later on, there was a smell of dinner in the corridors, and not many people felt up to that, but I did, as I had known I would. I sat in the saloon reading for hours, and felt the boat lifting me up and letting me fly between sea and sky before dropping me down, and it had no effect on me at all. I stood a long time out on deck with a firm grip on the rail, staring into the lashing grey and heard the wind howling in masts and cables, then I went inside with salt water in my hair, to the cafeteria where I sat down to talk with young Americans on their way through Europe to see a bit of the world just once before settling down, but they felt sick now and looked it too, and I laughed and said: "This is nothing."

I showed them the FNL badge and told them that the peasants with their round pointed hats and wide trousers would tear them to pieces in the end. I held out the Bobby Seale book so they could see the gloved fist on the cover, and I explained how the Black Panthers' fight with the American government was more than ripe and completely justified, and they looked at me with seasick eyes as if I had taken leave of my senses. But I had never felt more sensible, I was mental health personified, and I am sure I was laughing the whole voyage through, for I knew that when the boat finally reached its destination and glided quietly up the long Humber with its docks and fishing boats, past Grimsby on the way in to Hull where it would stop and moor up, then my brother would be on the quay waiting to share all that was his with me.

Now he lies behind a screen with his face to the wall refusing to talk to me, and he is all that I have, except perhaps for a nurse in green with a first name that begins with a G and a Kurd who can speak no Norwegian except "Hi" and "Thanks". Surely that cannot be right, but it feels like that when I drive into the garage under the block and park the Mazda with its bonnet against the wall in my corner so the neighbours will not see the big scrape along the front wing.

I go up the stairs to the ground floor and let myself in and undress in the bedroom with the radio on and I hear the Østland programme announcing that the world's most beautiful cat has run away from its owner in Stovner. It is large with ginger stripes and is the pride of the neighbourhood, says the presenter, and I get into bed and close my eyes and sleep until the telephone starts to ring. I open my eyes again. The room is dark now. The radio is still on and the alarm clock shows it is late evening. I get up and go into the living room over to the window while the telephone rings. It is raining a little between the blocks. I have no clothes on, but in the living room too it is dark so no-one can see in. There is light in Mrs Grinde's apartment. She stands by the dumb waiter with the telephone in her hand. That is what it looks like, at least at a distance, and my phone is still ringing. She turns and looks out of the window towards my apartment, and then she lowers her arm. The ringing stops. I stay there in front of the big window and she goes on standing in front of hers with a hand on what must be the telephone, and I am sure she is biting her lip and shifting her weight from foot to foot. Not impatiently, but restlessly maybe, at a loss.

I go back to the bedroom and switch the radio off and lie down under the duvet, close my eyes and try to go back to sleep. But it is no good. I try to think of nothing, but that doesn't work either, and then I just lie looking up into the darkness, thinking about my father. The Danish lady in his wallet. She was never mentioned. I try to recall what it was Aunt Solgunn told me: that he met her in Copenhagen a year before he got married when he went there with leave from the factory where he had been since he was fourteen. He was like the others in the family, with the exception perhaps of Uncle Alf, and never had a day's absence, if you don't count four days in hospital after a ski-jumping accident which turned his back into his weakest point, and now he had been given a grant to go and see how the Danes made shoes, whether he could learn something there, which he doubted, but still he was eager to go. There had been a fire at his factory, everything had to be rearranged and they were waiting for new machinery, and if he was to go, it had to be then. So they let him go, and when he was back he was sure they would make him foreman.

The first factory was owned by a co-operative run on

trade union lines, and the thing that struck him straight away was that the workers thought he was Swedish, and they did not understand what he said if he talked at his usual speed, although he understood *them* well enough. He thought that was funny and slightly irritating, for if my grandfather was Swedish, my father was *Norwegian*, and the biggest things for him after the establishment of the Norwegian Federation of Labour was Fridtiof Nansen's skiing journey across the Greenland ice and Roald Amundsen's victorious race to the South Pole. The second thing he noticed was that beer and schnapps were on sale at lunchtime in the canteen, where the workers played dice incessantly, and he thought that even more funny and quite exotic, even though he could not see how it might increase production. But they had music while they worked and ten minutes' obligatory exercise towards the end of the shift every single day. He like both things and he liked the idea of the workers having their own factory which supplied them with good shoes they could buy in their own shops all over the country and not the cheap shit he knew was on its way on to the market from places where they did not have a clue. And he liked the daughter of the assistant manager who was put in charge of him for the first week. He met her at the office on the second day, where she sat behind a desk and was a secretary with very smooth, shining blonde hair.

She talked efficiently on the telephone, her left hand drawing pictures in the air he had to follow with his eyes, and when she raised her head and said something in Danish he thought was the beginning of a song, he was a goner. Her father, the assistant manager, had once been a worker and later foreman, and after a few days my father thought if he just persevered and learned still more, nothing was impossible. He had thought that before, quite often, in fact, and time was running out. If it was to be done, it must be done now.

And there was something about him. He was reaching out. He was still shining. The assistant manager's daughter saw that at once. She kept her eyes on him all through the week he was at the factory, and when he went on to the next one, she kept in touch.

"I never give up," he solemnly said at the gate, "it is not in my nature," and then he laughed in his shy way, and she did not doubt him for a moment. Two weeks later they were secretly engaged, and when he left for home she promised to follow him soon to see what it was in his life that made him shine.

And she came. What she saw was grey rocks and ponderous spruce trees, and everything seemed suddenly so small and cramped about the narrow fjord where the forest shut out the sun, and she saw the little room where he lived alone at Number 1 Enebakkveien with the books he had bought by the greatest Norwegian authors and then some, perhaps to find something there that he could aspire to, but he never got through them. The books were dusty now, and then she would not know the titles of any of them. On the floor above were the premises of the Baptist Congregation where his father ruled like a patriarch over his family and a handful of workers whose souls had been saved, and she went out and looked at the shabby town which was not in the least like Copenhagen; no canal and golden domes, no great squares and extensive parks, no towering grandeur. But she saw the childish pride he took in all this, and her heart sank like a stone from summer to far below zero. She began to study train timetables and boat routes and presumably she said, as they used to say in B films of that era:

"Sorry, Buster, no deal," or something to that effect, and then she left after only a few days; quite quietly and unnoticed she went back to the assistant manager and the King's Town.

That night my father disappeared. There was to be a family gathering with all the brothers and sisters and their wives and husbands in honour of the Danish fiancée, which was no longer a secret. They wanted to see Frank Jansen finally crossing the finishing line. He was thirty-seven. But she did not come. Nor did he, and the next day he was not at work. It was a sensation. Nobody knew where he was, no-one could remember when they had actually seen him last, and after a day had passed they grew frightened and began to search. First among the friends he had, boxers and football players of the Olympic team in Berlin in 1936 which he never got to, although he had trained and trained, and then among those he knew in Bryn male voice choir, but he was not with any of them, and they searched in the cafés he went to from time to time to have a ginger ale and talk, and they were afraid he might be drunk although no-one had ever seen him drunk at any time. Finally, they organised a search party in the Østmark Forest. They carried on for three days, and the wind was howling and the rain came down as if Domesday was near, and still more and more people joined in; shoemakers and cross-country skiers, preachers and members of the choir, and one or two wrestlers with upper arms thick as birch trunks came rolling along, and they divided the forest into sections among themselves and walked past lakes and hills, up tortuous paths and down still more tortuous trails made by roe deer and elk. In the evenings they crowded together in the congregational hall with dripping clothes and spread maps out on the table in front of them where they ticked off the areas they had already covered, and next morning lorries trundled up to the parking place by the Østmark café, and from there they walked into the forest again. They shouted and sang baritone and bass through the rain that fell so heavily the voices were felled to the ground, and they shook their heads at each other, the water splashing off their sou'westers, the wet oilskins shining among the tree trunks when they flung out their arms in frustration, and they were close to giving up.

And then, on the third day, just before nightfall, the low sun broke through the steel-grey layer of clouds and sent a ray of light slanting down through the trees on to a solitary hut, and those among them who were Baptists saw it as a sign and went in. There he lay on a bunk sleeping like one dead, with the picture of the Danish fiancée clutched in one hand. He had not eaten for four days, his clothes were in rags, he had bruises on his face from his own fists, and they woke him, and he did not know where he was or what had happened.

"Has the referee counted to ten," he said. The men standing in the hut stroked their faces with sopping wet hands, and they looked at each other, fearing the worst, but he did recover, although he was never the same again.

Some months later he received a letter telling him he had a child in Denmark, in Jutland, with a lady he had met in a café near the factory and had spent a short time with the previous autumn, and who then just vanished. And it was not that he did not remember her, but it was more like a dream, for he had taken her to the cottage at Bunnefjord one night when the snow drifted past the walls and blew across the water, but inside it was warm and the night was warm, and when he woke up next morning she had gone and the snow had gone, and he did not see her again. Then his family kept on until she came alone on the Oslo boat, and after just a few days they went to the tabernacle together, and when they came out again they stopped on the pavement in the group of brothers and sisters, and he laughed and said: "Nailed to a cross on earth."

I am not sure now what Aunt Solgunn has told me and what I have made up myself, but what I think as I lie in the dark under the duvet looking up at the ceiling is that I would never have believed he was capable of it: passions, deep despair. All that. And would it have made any difference if it was something I had known while he lived?

"Without a doubt," I say aloud, "it would have made a great difference," and I know that is true, and nothing I can do or anything I can say will make time stop and go into reverse and make that difference less. And then the doorbell rings. I lie there listening. It does not ring again, but I am sure someone is standing outside waiting. I cannot ignore it now I have heard it, and maybe it is the Kurd on the third floor, perhaps he needs help again, perhaps the door to the stairwell is locked and he is standing in the rain without a key. I get up and put my trousers on and go out into the hall and open the door. Mrs Grinde is standing there. Her hair is wet. Her son is in her arms, swaddled in a woollen blanket. He is asleep with his head falling backwards. There are shining drops on his face. He does not look so bossy now.

"Hi," I say. She makes no reply. I stand there like an idiot, looking at her, and she bites her lip and gazes past me with the heavy boy in her arms, and I say:

"Do you want me to hold him for a bit?"

She shakes her head. Then I open the door wide and say:

"Come in, then."

Without hesitation, she walks past me, and that almost makes me scared. I do not know whether I can handle this. It is so long since anyone I have known in that way was here, two years in fact, that I do not remember what the form is, and with the boy it seems strangely intimate, almost like family. I do not know if I want family any more. It is too risky. I close the door, and follow her into the living room and say: "You can put him on the sofa."

And she does, she lays him down on the sofa very carefully with the woollen blanket tightly round his body, and he sleeps just as soundly. Slowly, she straightens her back as she takes off her coat and places it over the back of a chair, and then she turns towards me and runs her hand through her hair with her head on one side and says:

"I couldn't leave him alone."

"Of course not," I say.

"Why didn't you answer the phone?" she says. She is not wearing her glasses, but she does not peer either. How did she know I was here and could pick up the telephone?

"Do you wear contact lenses?" I say, and then she blushes quite visibly although the light is not on, and she faintly nods, and I say:

"I don't know. I do not know why I did not answer the phone. So many people call. It keeps on ringing." That is not really true, but it is true that I don't know why.

"You were quite visible though, standing there, in the light from the pathway," she says and smiles for the first time and now I am the one to blush. How many other people saw me? The naked man on stairwell F. She takes the few steps towards me, lifts her hand and places it lightly on my chest.

"You looked good," she says, and then leans forward and lays her head just as lightly over her hand and says:

"I am taking a chance here." Her hair tickles my chest and her mouth tickles, I am well aware I am standing here in my trousers and nothing else, and it is perfectly quiet and dark around us. Only the boy breathing on the sofa, and I cautiously place an arm round her shoulders, not committing myself.

"I know," I say. "You are brave."

"You were brave too, last night."

"That was different. I was sick then, and cold and

bombed out of my mind. Maybe I still am. I don't know. Last night is a long time off."

"Is it?" she says.

"Yes," I say. "Just about everything has happened since then." I feel her hand grow stiff, she starts to push, and then I tighten my grasp of her shoulder and hold her fast, and say:

"Why did you look at your watch, out there by the hospital?"

She grows softer in my arm and laughs deep down in her throat.

"That was so silly. I saw you standing there in front of the main entrance, and then I thought, is there time to go up to him for a moment, I just wanted a look at your face, and then, instinctively, I glanced at my watch. I didn't even see what time it was. It was just daft, we had a man to save."

"It was half past four," I say. "How is the man doing?"

"He died on the way in. He'd had a collision in the fog on the motorway. His chest was crushed against the wheel."

There is not much I can say to that, and I really do not feel like saying anything, so I just go on standing with my arm tightly round her shoulder, and it is a fine shoulder, and it fits me well, not being a tall man. Everything is almost perfect. I feel her relax with her cheek on my neck, and her breath tickling, and her hair too, and I stand waiting for the feeling that will push me on, for the ball is in my court now, I know the next step, and it is no more than right. But the feeling does not come. I do not know what is wrong. Perhaps it is the boy on the sofa.

"Why don't you ask why I was at the hospital?" I say.

"Because I know. I found out," she mumbles.

I see. She has found out, and now that she knows why I was at the hospital, she will give me the comforting hug. But she does not, she stands quietly without changing position, just breathes on my neck and she is not here to comfort me, but to get what she is entitled to, and I am all with her there, and we cannot go on like this for many more seconds before something happens. I do not know what to do. Then I suddenly remember the film about Zorba the Greek, the scene where Anthony Quinn bawls out the Englishman Alan Bates because he has committed the greatest sin a man can possibly commit. He had made a pass at the proud widow and succeeded, and perhaps she gave him a chance because he was different, but when it came to the crunch he had not the courage to go through that door she held open for him, and that stripped her bare and cost her her life.

I bend down slightly and put an arm round her back and the other behind her knees, and pick her up with a jerk. She clings to my neck, giggling.

"What on earth are you doing?"

"I am Zorba," I say.

"What?" she asks, but I do not reply. I walk across the room with Mrs Grinde in my arms, thinking: let the brain take the first step; and on the way into the bedroom I feel her weight like a tugging in the pit of my stomach, and then the feeling is there. I laugh aloud and shout:

"Here comes Zorba, make way, make way," and I lay her down on the bed not quite as elegantly as I had planned, and it is like a lousy film we both enjoy, although Zorba is not a lousy film. I stroke her hair and undress her as carefully as I possibly can, and she says:

"You don't have to be *that* chivalrous," and I reply:

"Oh, but I do," and under her clothes there are other garments she would never have worn on an everyday evening, and there is no doubt they are meant for me. That makes me pretty shaky and even sad, for she certainly *has* taken a chance, and I do not know if this is something I am able to receive, this boy she has carried in her arms past all the windows in the block, these clothes or rather lack of clothes right next to her skin, and she sees what I am looking at and blushes and bites her lip and refuses to meet my eyes and almost gets angry. Then I sink to my knees with my hands on *her* knees and a lump in my throat, and if it is not like it was last night it still is great and even more, for Christ's sake, and afterwards she lies quite still listening for sounds from the living room. But all is

164

quiet there too, the boy is sleeping, and she turns to me
with her face aflame and says:

"Tell me some more about your father."

"There's not much more to tell."

"Isn't there?"

"No."

"I must have missed something," she says.

11

The last time I spoke to him was on the telephone. He had been ill. It was cancer, but the operation had been successful and he was better now. He called on a Thursday, I was at work in the bookshop where I was still employed. We rarely talked to each other on the phone, and the few times it happened it was usually I who called my mother to give a message or to ask her advice, and it was he who picked up the receiver. Then it would not take him long to pass it over to her.

Now he said:

"Hi there, this is Dad. How is the writer doing?" And then he laughed, embarrassed, before stopping abruptly.

He was seventy-eight, I was thirty-seven, and it was so strange hearing him that I just stood there behind the counter with the phone in my hand, gazing into the air. There were books everywhere and lots of people, but I saw nothing. You had a very strange expression on your face, said my colleagues later.

"Hi," I said. "Well," I said, "not so bad." Around me were boxes of books sent all the way from America, and the books were all by Raymond Carver. He had died

166

two years before of lung cancer at just fifty years old, and we were going to have a memorial exhibition of all the titles published in stylish new editions. I had one of them in my hand. It was called *Where I'm Calling from*.

"Where are you calling from?" I asked.

"I'm at home," he said. "I'm standing here in the hall." And I saw him standing there in the hall with the striped wallpaper in white and gold I thought was tasteless, and I had thought so since I lived at home almost twenty years earlier. He stood by the mirror and the small table with its open drawer and the telephone directory open at T in front of him, for he could not remember the number of my workplace although I had been there for ten years. Before that I had been a workman like him for six years, but that was by my own choice, whereas he never had a choice.

It was just before Easter. On Saturday they were going down to Denmark by ferry as usual, but there had been a mistake over the tickets, he said, and sounded bewildered. They had been made out for this particular boat, but now that had been sold to the Swedes as a dormitory for refugees, and there was to be another one. He did not even know what it was called. When he called the firm and asked, they were as confused as he was at the other end of the line. Was there going to be a boat at all? Did I know anything about it? And wasn't I supposed to go with them?

I had forgotten that. I *was* supposed to go with

them. My mother had called me one morning and said:

"Now you just come along. I will pay for your ticket if it's a question of money."

"I have my own money," I said.

There were things they had to bring with them, and things that must be done in the spring, heavy things he could not manage any more; the old willow hedge needed clipping, a spruce tree must have its roots cut off and be pulled down with a rope and later chopped up and stacked for logs. Other things had to be taken away, and they had no car, nor a driving licence.

"Your father is an old man now," she said, "do you understand what I'm saying? I do not want him to do it all on his own." But he had always been old and he had always been strong, and on the few occasions I tried to help him he just pushed me aside and said:

"This is nothing."

That was not even true, goddamnit. That much I had learned. Everything was *some*thing. Just ask Basho.

But now I said:

"Sure, OK, I will come, I will bring the girls," and not until later did I realise that my two younger brothers were supposed to come too. That *they* could have dealt with the job, if it was help he wanted. That she might have had other reasons for putting pressure on me. And then I forgot all about it. Raymond Carver filled my days.

"Hello, are you still there?" I said.

"Yes, I'm here," he said.

"Something has come up," I said, "I can't get away before Monday." That was a sheer lie, and I knew as I spoke that I wished it unsaid, for the fact that *he* was the one to call really touched me. I do not know why, he had never touched me before, not that I could remember. But I had no possible way of getting tickets in two days, not for the Saturday before Palm Sunday. And now I really wanted to go. I could feel it. I don't know what came over me.

"But then I will come," I said. "I have borrowed a car and will go via Gothenburg. I am sure the problem with those tickets will sort itself out. They must have got hold of a boat since you have not heard otherwise."

"Oh, well, they probably have," he said, still with that hesitant voice old men have when they lose their sense of direction, but the conversation had ended, so we both understood. I was certain he knew I had lied, and at that moment it was not a nice feeling.

Two days later I was woken by the telephone. It was seven o'clock. I should have been up already.

"Switch on the TV," the voice said, and then there was a click, and all I heard was the dialling tone. I did not catch whose voice had spoken, but it had to be someone I knew. Asleep beside me in bed lay the woman whose face I have forgotten, and the girls slept in their rooms with the light full on their faces. I rose and went into the living room and put the TV on. It was tuned to Sweden. The test image played, so I changed channel to NRK. The screen flickered, and suddenly there was a boat there on the open sea quite alone, filmed from the air, first from the one side and then the whole way round from the other, from in front and behind in continuous circles. A helicopter, I thought, and listened for the flapping sound of the rotor blades, but I heard nothing. It was morning and grey dawn, the sea was calm and blue, the boat was blue and white, and everything was quiet and a bit confusing. I had never seen that boat before. I was tired. I had been drunk the night before. I did not get the point. But there was smoke coming from the boat, white smoke and black smoke that rose in a column to the sky and spread and lay like a filter against the light, and the helicopter turned and flew down as low as it could get, and then I saw flames break out from the windows along the whole of one side and from the aft deck many metres up in the air. I did not see any people, but I saw the name of the boat. It was a nice name, a suitable name. And suddenly my feet felt icy cold. A paralysing cold which hurt, and I stared at the screen, I turned up the sound and heard the voice from the studio telling me why precisely that boat was on television so early on a Saturday morning, on April 7, 1990. The paralysis rose from my feet up my thighs to the hips, and then I could not stand on my feet any more, there was something quite wrong with my legs, I've got MS, I thought, it's a wheelchair from now on, and then I slid down on the sofa and grabbed the telephone I had in the living room and dialled my brother's number without taking my eyes off the screen.

"Hello," he said wearily.

"Switch on the TV," I said. He switched his TV on, keeping hold of the telephone. I heard the voice from the studio in the room he was in. I heard him breathe, but he said nothing.

"I should have been on that boat," I said, "but I forgot, you know, I just forgot about it, and then it was too late. If I had not forgotten it, if I had just gone with them, then nothing would have happened."

"Oh, God," he said, his voice completely flat, "please, be quiet, please."

I wake up once, and it is night. I must have gone on talking in my sleep, my lips are still moving and they feel swollen, and there is an echo of words in a hollow in my head. I raise my hand and run it over my face. It is soaking wet again. There is a pain in my side, and something in my throat burns and irritates. I cautiously clear it. Someone is breathing in the darkness beside me as if nothing has happened, as if life has stood still, and for a moment I do not remember who it is and panic and switch on the light over the bed. She smiles in her sleep and puts her arm over her eyes and turns, not away from me but towards me, and the relief I feel is overwhelming. I turn off the light and go back to sleep, and dream that my brother has made himself a fortune out of insurance shares and bought himself a sailing boat.

"We, the rich, have it made," he says, "I wouldn't have been poor for all the money in the world."

We are on board that boat, just him and me, and there is a fresh breeze out past Færder lighthouse in the wake of bigger boats, and we lie so low in the water that you only have to lean over the gunwale to get a handful of foaming salt water. And I do that, I lean over the gunwale and scoop up the water in my hands and rinse my face and get some in my mouth and swallow and think: it has a new taste, it was not like this before. Then I tease my brother about his new sailing shoes, which only upper-class people use, in my opinion. I would not touch a pair like that even if someone paid me to.

"Is tennis the next thing then, or what?" I ask and laugh through clenched teeth – "or golf maybe, or buy slalom skis and mix with the in-crowd?"

"But it was Dad who made them," he says through tears, "he wanted me to have them."

"That is not true," I say.

*

That dream plunges me into such despair that I wake

up. I lie stiffly, holding my breath, and there is not a sound in the room. I am alone. I slide my arm over the pillow, it is still warm, but she has not left a note. I do not want to be alone. I jump out of bed and run into the hall. In the mirror I see a face, and I stop and without thinking grab the first thing I see, a metal box standing on the chest, and hurl it at the mirror. The glass breaks with an incredibly loud noise, it disintegrates into glittering fragments raining silver on the floor, and I stand there watching them spread all over the hall like the aftermath of an explosion in a film on TV. One of the fragments slices into my arm and blood trickles out, not much but enough to show red against the white skin. I raise my arm and lick the blood up, and then I hop slalom between the glass splinters into the living room. The boy has gone from the sofa, only the impression in the cushions reveals he was there. I run over to the big window gasping for breath, hand to my side, and I stop close to it with my nose on the glass, and stare across to the next block. She is standing at her window in her dressing gown. I am as naked as I was the previous time, and I see her turning and looking back at me, and we just stand there and then she lets her dressing gown drop without thinking of those who may be awake, as we are awake, and can see her from this side. Her skin shines dimly and is whiter than anything else I can see, and she lifts both hands and lays their palms against the pane, and then I do the same, lift my hands and lay the palms against the pane, and it's as if it was just that one window, a few millimetres of glass between her and me on a night when the rain has stopped and the moon hangs transparent and clear above the block right in front of me, and I stand naked in my own living room with hands and nose on the window, and I hear my breath wheezing and my heart beating, but otherwise all is silence.

I do not know how long we stand like this, perhaps a minute, perhaps five minutes, but then it is over. She raises one hand and covers her face, and with the other makes a movement meant only for me, that most people would call indecent indeed, and I know she is laughing, and she waves and I wave back and then she is gone.

It will soon be morning, but I go back to bed and sleep until the day is far advanced. I have no dreams I can remember when I wake up, but I am sweating under the duvet and have a headache. There is sunshine in the room. The air is thick, and I get up and open the window and look straight out to the path and the space in front of the block where the usual ladies walk past with the usual kids in rather lighter clothes today on their way to the playground or on their way back, and it is late March and suddenly warm. The men I see are refugees from very different parts of the world, and they do not play with their children as I might have done just a few years ago in front of this very block, no, they stand quite still and rigid by the sandpit with their hands in their pockets or arms crossed on their chest, with a stiff smile round their mouth and a dreaming expression in their eyes looking right through the blocks and far, far away.

A couple of Norwegian men who are on social security walk past very slowly with a slight but pronounced limp. It is wasted on me, I have no reason to doubt their disability. It is *mine* I doubt. When one of the neighbours had seen me staying at home for the third month on end, he came up to me one day at the Co-op and asked timidly:

"So, are you on benefit now?"

"No," I said, "I am on a scholarship," and he gave a sympathetic nod, understanding it was something to do with my nerves.

"Well, it's not easy," he said.

"No," I said, "it's not."

He stayed at home himself, and told me he did not dare go shopping before the middle of the day. I took his point. That was a couple of years ago. After that we have greeted each other like two men with a fate in common. Now I see him walking along the path on his way to the Co-op, so it must be late.

I go from the open bedroom window through the hall close to the wall as carefully as I can and into the living room where the desk is tidy and dusted with the little Mac switched off and quiet. Beside it lies a not particularly thick pile of typescript. I put on my spectacles and riffle lightly through the pile, and it seems as if I had not seen it before, page after page with unreadable, indifferent writing, from a world no longer mine. If it ever was. I pick up the pile from the table and walk into the kitchen and throw everything into the plastic bag beneath the sink. Two years straight into the bin. I feel neither one thing nor another. I take the plastic bag out and tie the drawstring and go back to the living room, switch the Mac on, wait, click on "hard disk" and get the menu, then use the mouse to log on to the file named "new book" and drag it round the whole screen to the waste bin in the bottom right-hand corner. It always makes me think of the first Fleetwood Mac LP I bought in 1968 when Peter Green was young and his brain not yet bombed. *I've got a hellhound on my trail*, it sings inside of me, the bin bulges and widens in the middle, and I find the icon for "empty waste bin". "Click," I say aloud and push my index finger down, and the waste bin gets slim again. Then I find the file with the few sentences I wrote some days ago, which run: *I see the shape of the wind on the water*, and switch on the printer to make a copy. I click off and close down, pick up the one sheet and put it in the top drawer. Brush invisible dust from the table top. Get up. That was that. Now I must go out.

I put my boots on and lace them up, then the pea

jacket with only a T-shirt underneath, trying not to look down at the floor still covered with glass splinters. I pick up the rubbish bag and stuff the dog-eared, much-read edition of *100 Haiku* in Norwegian in my pocket, and then I go out and lock the door and throw the bag down the rubbish shaft, and on my way through the entrance hall I open the letter box. There lies *The Class Struggle* and two letters. One is from my publisher. Not long ago I would have torn it open at once and gone to sit by myself to read in peace, but now I leave it all where it is, shut the box and go out into the sunshine. It is Friday, I think. The blocks lie in a row shutting out the view, and further up there are terraced houses for those who can afford them and want to get on in the world and have a little lawn they can mow. Some think that important. It will soon be time for the annual voluntary spring-cleaning. Then we must all go out together on the caretaker's orders to sweep the paths and hose away refuse and dog mess and plant shrubs and paint the fence in front of two square metres of grass on each side of the entrance doors, and though there is not one of us who gives a damn, we have to chat. I simply hate it. I do not know anyone any more, do not know who lives on my stair apart from Naim Hajo although I am the one who has been here longest. No-one in their right mind stays for more than three years.

But at least the sun is shining. The windows sparkle and it's not nearly as warm as it seemed inside the apartment. I am glad about that. I walk the pathway further up the hill through the neutral zone that divides the area between blocks and terraced houses, and the nursery school is just opposite the small football pitch. All the children are outside. I stop by the fence and stand watching them at play, and see G's boy on top of a sand heap in a thick jumper and waterproof trousers. He is talking loudly, he waves a little red spade and points. He knows what he wants. He is the boss. And then he notices me standing there watching him, and he has no idea we have been twice in combat, that he was beaten both times, at home and away both. I nod to him with a slight smile, I feel obliged to, and he looks straight at me, and he does not know who I am. He makes a face and then sticks his tongue out. The little bastard. I laugh and shake my head. He is suitably miffed and turns his back and with his little spade starts to shovel sand with great force.

I walk away from the fence and up to the summit where the terraced houses have the finest view of the forest and the valley and all that is nice, and their hedges and lawns will soon be subjected to a strict ritual before spring breaks out in earnest, and right at the top I drop down below the road on a pathway leading into the forest on the other side. The whole time I have had eyes on my back from windows and doorways, and although it has not been as bad as it usually is I stop in the semi-darkness beneath the little bridge to rest and roll a cigarette before deciding whether to turn and go back the same way or take the road round the whole housing area or perhaps some other way altogether. I can go from here and get on to the ancient paths and walk there for days, seeing no other houses than long-forgotten smallholdings with their buildings falling down or crumbled long ago and after that just the occasional log cabin. That is what the neighbours say. I have lived here for fourteen years and never been further in than a few hundred metres to collect fir cones when the girls were quite small and fascinated by small things.

I stand smoking in the shadow of the little concrete bridge, watching the sun shining on the spruces closest by and on the path that bends and disappears behind a cliff. A cluster of birches filters the light in yellow and shining black through its bare branches, and it looks like a magazine illustration or an old print from China or Japan, and I could have hung that picture on my wall. So why not? I finish my smoke and stub the butt out with the toe of my boot and start walking. I turn twice and look back, and the houses are still there, but the third time they have gone. I try to recall the last time I could not see a house or was close to one or inside one, and it must be long since.

I remember one house I was in. I lay on the sofa in the living room trying to recover, I might have been to a party the night before and I felt worn out and left out,

I had no family any more, everything was lost. Then my father came downstairs. I knew his step from all others, the weight of him, and he walked past me across the floor to the window and pulled the curtain aside. A faint light came in.

"The fog is lifting," he said. "We must get going. They are on your trail." I turned and saw the light on his face, a soft grey light, like invisible smoke in the room. He was as old as I am now, and what he said did not frighten me, for he was keeping watch and knew what we had to do. But there wasn't much time, I had to pull myself together.

It must have been a dream, of course, because I do not remember what that house looked like from outside or what he saw from the windows or why we were actually there. I remember a lot of dreams. Sometimes they are hard to distinguish from what has really happened. That is not so terrible. It is the same with books.

I walk a kilometre or two over easy slopes both up and down, and then the path bends steeply towards the top of a knoll. I really have to make my legs work, and though my breathing is not that good, the going is better than expected and that makes me enthusiastic. I could have had a dog like Glahn has in Hamsun's *Pan*, and it could have bounded in front of me along this path and its name could be Aesop or Lyra, and each time a person or an animal was going to cross our path it would warn me at once so I could retreat among the trees and watch them pass, and the dog would sit there obediently at my feet. I could have had a gun and lived on what I managed to shoot, small game and large birds, and lived in a cabin with the few things I needed: some books, an old-fashioned typewriter, clothes for all seasons and enough dry firewood, I could have been a Tibetan monk, I could have been someone completely different from the person I am, of course, but I am not, and when I get to the top of the knoll and there is a view, I see forest whichever way I turn. Far down to the right is a long narrow lake, and from where I stand I cannot see where it begins or ends. There is ice on the lake with open patches, and I would not have tried to walk on that ice. In the shadows on the other side there is snow on the slope. There ought to have been an elk walking beside that lake, but there is no elk in sight, and everything is quiet, nothing moves but a thin wisp of smoke from some place deeper into the forest.

I sit down by a rock with a view of the lake and roll a cigarette, and when it's lit I take the book of haiku from my pocket. It is a long time since I read it, but I leaf through and find the poem about the night falling on to the road where no-one walks, and I read it a couple of times and then some more poems, and then one about a willow tree that paints the wind without a brush, and I know willows well from Denmark where you can see them everywhere and there is always a wind, and I can picture it clearly. I close the book and put out the cigarette and look across the lake to the thin wisp of smoke that still hangs there above the forest some miles away and barely moves, and then I close my eyes and rest my head against the rock with the sun on my face and sleep for a while. When I wake what I remember is just something about the wind and a white house by the water.

On the way home I call in at the Co-op and buy the things I did not get yesterday. I just make it before closing time, and in truth I buy rather more than I need, and then I walk up the pathway with the bag in my hand. Clouds have come up and it is cold again, but not *that* cold. I see no-one in front of the block. Inside the hall I take my post from the letter box, and when I get to my door, Naim Hajo, the Kurd from the second floor, is ringing my doorbell. He has a book under his arm.

"Hi," I say, and he says:

"Hi" with a smile, and I unlock the door, push it open and make a slight bow with one arm out. The arm trembles, and I do not know why. Perhaps because I have forgotten to eat again. He does not miss that.

"Go on in," I say. And so he does, takes a step across the threshold, then stops short and looks at the splinters of glass sparkling like a carpet right over to the living-room door, and he looks at me and grows serious. He points at the floor with an enquiring look on his face.

"That's nothing," I say.

He looks as if he understands what I say, and he looks as if he does not agree. Perhaps he has read Basho. He shakes his head and says: "Problem." Just like that. And then he points at me, and not at my face, rather at where my heart is. I consider whether I have a problem in that area, but there is none that I can explain to him, not in the language he and I use. What I have is a broken mirror. But I know I am glad he is concerned. And he has three words now. That almost elates me.

"One moment," I say and stop him with my hands. I fetch a brush and a dustpan and sweep a way for us through the glass splinters from the front door to the living room, and I wave him on.

"Come on in," I say. "Coffee?" I ask, and he smiles and understands that word well without any trouble and follows me into the kitchen. I indicate one of the chairs with my hand, and he sits down and takes the book from under his arm and places it on the table in front of the brass bowl. The bowl glitters newly polished in the light from the window. I can see it makes him pleased. I am pleased too. I take the groceries out of the shopping bag and spread them out on the worktop, and for want of something more oriental I make some ferociously strong coffee with the

Co-op's green brand, the way I hope he will like it. Fortunately there is a clean cloth on the table, and I lay cups and bowls and plates from the same service, the finest I have, which I inherited from my mother, who brought it with her from Denmark in the early fifties. Suddenly the way everything looks seems important, that everything is for real, and that *he* understands that, because in *his* part of the world the drinking of coffee is more than filling a mug and taking it out on the balcony. After all, I am not completely ignorant. I pour milk into a small jug and put sugar in a matching bowl, and find two teaspoons that are actually silver. I get a packet of oatcakes from the shopping bag, tear it open and take out a suitable number and spread them with light margarine, put them in a small basket that someone who once lived here left behind, and for a moment I wonder whether to light some candles. But I do not have any candles, and anyway it is the middle of the day, and with candles it might have looked like a rendezvous.

When there is nothing more to be done, I sit down and pour out his coffee and wait until he has helped himself to sugar and stirred with the spoon and taken the first mouthful. He nods and smiles. That is a proper cup of coffee, is what he thinks, and I fill my own cup and have a taste.

"A bit on the strong side if you ask me," I say, "but then I am Norwegian." and he is with me, whether he understands what I say or not, and I take a biscuit and he takes a biscuit, and we chew and drink coffee for a while without saying anything, and then I remember the dream of the house I was in with my father, that they were after me, and that he helped me get out before it was too late.

"Is your father alive?" I ask, then wait before saying:

"*My* father is dead. That's not so strange, he would have been more than eighty now and maybe dead no matter what had happened. It is really much worse than the others are dead. But the odd thing is that it took me six years to realise it is unbearable. Can you understand that?" I say, shaking my head, and he points at me and says:

"Problem," and I do not deny it. When you run naked through your hall in the night and on impulse smash the wall mirror into powder, you do have a small problem, that goes without saying. I nod and openly admit it, and he points to his own heart.

"Problem," he says again. And I can understand that. He is thousands of miles from the place where he has lived for most of his life, and perhaps he has a father in a village in the far north of Iraq and he will never see him again, or that father is dead, and someone did kill him, and then he comes here, and the first word he learns is "thanks" and the third is "problem". Then "hi" in the middle is not of much help. I nod again.

"I *have* seen you at night, you know," I say. He cocks his head and looks at me enquiringly, and then I put my face in my hands and rock my body back and forth, and while I am doing this I realise I may have gone too far. I cautiously glance up at him. His eyes are shining and he strokes his moustache again and again, but he nods. Very slightly. I hasten to fill up his cup and pass him the basket of oatcakes. He is polite and takes some and has a mouthful of coffee, and then he puts his hand on the book and pushes it towards me and then opens his hands. I am to receive yet another gift. It is too much, really. I turn it over and see it is *Memed, my Hawk* by Yasar Kemal. I remember well when I read it fifteen years ago. Remember the chair I was sitting in and the colour of the curtains and the colours of the paint on the walls in the apartment in Bjølsen where I lived then, and the humming sound of buses on their way in to the roundabout outside my windows and the brakes at the bus stop and the doors opening. Remember the Irish music I played each day that became linked for ever with the burning thistles on the Tsjukorova plain and the stockings that Memed's sweetheart knitted in a unique pattern meant especially for him. And I remember who gave me that book, and that I asked if she could knit a pair of stockings like that for me. And she did, as well as she could from Kemal's description in the book. And suddenly her face is back, and the years when I saw that face, and the scent of her and the way she walked, and the way she ran her fingers through her hair to push it away from her eyes, and then the face again as it was in the labour ward twice with me on my knees by her bed, and once more as it was at the end, distorted and furious, and at once my throat starts to hurt. I desperately clear it and stand up, I take his hand and say:

"Thanks," and I cough again. "Just a moment," I say and put down the book and leave the table and walk through the living room to the bathroom in the hall. There I turn on the tap and put the plug in and let the water fill the basin more than halfway up. I take a deep breath and hold it down and bend and push my face into the water. It is icy cold, but I stand like that until I have to breathe. This time I dry my face thoroughly in a big towel hanging on the wall. I run my hands through my hair and look at myself in the mirror. I do not know whom I resemble any more. Then I go back. He sits on his chair and has not moved. He looks at me, and I know what he is going to say. I nod.

"Problem," I say. No question.

12

Time slides into April. It is spring, no doubt about it. I reread books. I have made a list of the twenty I have liked the best, and after several sittings it is down to ten. *Memed, my Hawk* is one of them. I am looking for something, but I do not know what.

My brother is discharged from hospital after a short stay in the psychiatric ward in the basement, the bunker, as it is called. I do not visit him. There is no point, and anyway they cannot give him any help there that he would accept. So he does not stay long, and when he gets home he is into divorce proceedings at once. I talk to Randi on the telephone. She is the one who calls me.

"He is completely apathetic," she says. "He doesn't give a damn. Won't you talk to him?"

What am I to say to that? She likes to fight, and now there is no resistance. That makes her confused and angry. But it is not my problem.

"Just get it over with," I say.

"It shouldn't be *that* easy," she says.

"Oh, yes, it should," I say. "Here today, gone tomorrow. That's how it is."

*

She moves out one Saturday, with David and a good deal more, and then he is alone in the big empty house on Fetsund. He buys her share of the house, and that cleans him out and then some. The house is mortgaged up to the hilt.

I call him on April 7, early in the day. He is at home on sick leave.

"Hello," he says.

"Hi," I say, "it's me. Your brother. You'll remember me if you search your mind. It is a kind of jubilee today, is it not. Want to go for a beer?"

"Your treat?"

"Sure thing."

"OK," he says. "Can you pick me up? She took the car."

"If *my* car will start, I will."

It does, of course, it never lets me down. Give me any car at all, as long as it's Japanese and begins with an m and ends with an a. I have replaced the scratched bumper with one from a scrapyard, and it is really posh, and even has the same paint colour as the original.

I drive down the hills to Lillestrøm, cross the bridge over the Nitelva and in through the first streets past the station. All the snow has gone, not a patch to be seen on the way down. There are coltsfoot beside the

189

roadside ditches, the April sun is shining, and the workers on the new railway to Gardermoen airport wear orange trousers and white T-shirts that are still quite clean. They are laying rails with huge machines and signal to each other with gloved hands. The gloves are yellow and can be seen from a long way off. I catch myself singing "Somewhere" from *West Side Story*, and not quite like in the original version by Leonard Bernstein, but more like Tom Waits on the *Blue Valentine* LP from before he stopped smoking. To my ears it sounds quite similar, but I'm not sure everyone would support that view. "There's a place for us," I bellow in a gurgling voice, and then I start coughing. I ought to stop smoking myself. My father would have liked that. Or maybe not. It would have made him less unique among us, with his body like a temple; no whited sepulchres in sight. His temple got cancer, but that can happen to anyone; a genetic time bomb placed there by chance at birth, ticking and running, and then one day: Bang. If that happens to me it will be far from chance. That is the difference between us, and it is a big difference.

But I feel better now than I have for a long time. I do.

They are building a new railway station beside the old one in Lillestrøm, and it looks good. I like railway stations made of glass and steel, I like airports, I like big bridge spans and concrete constructions if they are bold enough, I can drive long diversions to see a power station in the mountains or in the depths of a valley, I like high-tension cables in straight lines through the landscape, and presumably that is because I read too many Soviet novels at a certain age. Light over the land, that is what we want. Light in every lamp, light in every mind.

I drive out of Lillestrøm following the roundabouts by Åråsen football stadium where LSK plays its home matches, but I have never liked LSK in their canary-yellow colours, have never been into that ground, only heard the heart-rending jubilation when Vålerenga gets knocked out again and again, and then I turn out on to the road to Fetsund and step on the gas to about ninety kilometres an hour straight over the big plain where the rivers meet and break their banks at the end of spring every single year when the melt water from the mountains comes down through the valleys and all the way here. Sometimes the cattle stand in the meadows beside the highway with water above their hocks in the mist looking like water buffalo in films from the Yangtze, Mekong; I remember women on bicycles in round pointed hats with grenades on the handlebars and grenades in their carriers in the rain and the water up to the hubs on their way through the forest to the front.

"Jesus, they're all so good-looking," my friend Audun said when we sat there in the packed hall at college. The black-and-white images flickered in our faces and lit up the FNL badges we wore on our lapels. We were eighteen, and in the dark all hands were raised to stroke the shiny emblems.

That was twenty-five years ago, I have not seen Audun for fifteen. I guess he has got along all right. We do get along, in some way or other.

When the plain is behind me, the road rises steeply to the ridge in a long hill before swooping over the top and then going down on the other side and out on to the big bridge over the Glomma River. Far down on the right the old timber booms shine in the sun and cut the water up into squares, and the little red lumberjacks' cabins float above the river where before you could hear the cries of command and the sound of singing and arrogant laughter right up until I was twenty years and more, and the dull boom of log hitting log filled the dreams of many, and many risked their life balancing with only a few inches of soapy smooth timber between their boot soles and the icy cold flood water for the sake and profit of the forest barons. Now everything is newly painted and nice looking and as quiet as a museum. Not one person in sight. The water is almost green and flows massively under the bridge and heavily out into the vast lake. It heaves and bulges, full of itself.

On the other side of the bridge I just start up the next hill before turning right by the Hydro station and in past the county hall and the school. His house is straight ahead with a view of the river through the trees. It is a dark bluish-red in colour; and he designed it himself. That was his dream, to pull himself out of the terraced houses and apartment blocks and to live in a house that was built to his own design, and now he does, alone. The tracks of a car show on the gravel in front of the door. I park in the tracks to fill the vacancy and switch the ignition off. I wait in the car. Some stay inside when they hear a car and wait until the doorbell rings, while others hear the car and come out on to the steps to welcome their visitor. My brother has always been of the latter. But no-one comes out. Perhaps he is at the shop. It is not too far for him to walk. I wait for a few moments. Suddenly I get anxious and push the car door open and get out and run across the gravel to the entrance. The door is not locked, so I go on into the hall which is almost as big as the hall in an American soap on television, and I run straight downstairs to the room in the basement with the big windows on to the river. What was once a television room is now filled with cardboard boxes. The walls are bare. The room seems enormous. There is nothing in it apart from a small stereo outfit and an easel in front of one window, and my brother stands at the easel with a brush in his hand and headphones on his curly head. He does not notice me and I stand there behind him and see what he is painting is the island with the lighthouse just off the coast of Denmark where our cabin is. He must have a photograph somewhere. So do I, I think. He is painting the childhood horizon. His childhood, and mine.

He is thinner. He used to look like a bear, while I have been more like a fox, and now he is pretty close to an elk, and I glimpse the brother I once went to see in Hull when everything in life was still before us and nothing was settled yet. We may be closer to that point than we have ever been during the years in between. I could wish for that. But I am not sure. I feel nervous, there is something about that slim back, and then he turns quite calmly and is not surprised to see me standing there. He must have realised the whole time and just gone on with what he was doing, and that certainty does not reassure me. His face is thinner too, and he smiles crookedly with a new glint in his eye. He knows something I do not know. He takes off the headphones and I can hear it is Steve Earle he is playing: "I've been to hell, and now I'm back again. I feel all right."

"What do you think?" he asks and gestures at the easel. I look at the picture. It is good. It is very good. It is exactly as I imagine it; glimmering, floating, for ever shut.

"You have always been a good painter," I say.

"It is a long time since I did anything. I have been at it for several days. You know where it is?"

I nod. "Oh, yes," I say.

"What do you think when you look at it?" he asks. His face is crushingly calm. His eyes have dark shadows. I am not sure if I like him like this. Why does he suddenly have to ask me about that now?"

"I think all that has gone to hell," I say.

"I don't."

"Good for you," I say.

I have often talked tough to him, felt free to do so as his little brother, but never like this, sharp, bitter. Something in his expression provokes me, the serenity he shows, and his new appearance, as if he has seen the Light. A quarter of an hour ago I felt quite good myself, but now my heart is in my mouth. In a few minutes only our roles have reversed. There is an itch at my back and he smiles just as calmly and looks at me with that look, puts his brush in a jar and wipes his hands on a rag. Out of the window behind him I see a boat on the river, it pounds against the current and barely moves forward until it gives up and turns in a big arc towards the opposite shore and suddenly puts on speed and disappears.

"Well, it is," he says, peering at me.

"Shall we go?" I ask.

"I just have to go up for a shower and a change. Get cleaned up."

"Undoubtedly," I say.

"It's the seventh of April, Arvid. Cut it out," he says without raising his voice.

I take a deep breath. "OK," I say.

We both glance at the picture, and then walk up the stairs to the ground floor. He goes first and I follow, and his steps are not as heavy as they used to be, and he walks on up to the first floor while I go into the kitchen and sit down by the specially designed table. Here almost everything is unchanged. Solid and simple with few colours and a lot of polished metal, like a ship's galley or a communal kitchen, only much more expensive. The floor is composed of unusually wide planks, brought here from a sawmill in Høland. Even the door handles are masculine, Randi used to say. It was not really her style, but he had it all planned in beforehand. Now she can do as she likes, and I am certain she will. I roll a cigarette and get up to find an ashtray. That's not easy, neither of them smokes, and neither of them liked me to when I came to visit. But then I have not been to see them much since they moved to this place. I get a saucer from the cupboard and sit down at the table to wait and smoke and look at the river. There are no boats on it now. Only the sun on the flowing green water and the booms on the other side.

When he comes downstairs he has showered and changed his clothes. They hang on him a bit, and his belt has more holes than it has had for twenty years. With his damp hair combed back the thinness of his face is even more obvious. He looks many years younger or perhaps just different. It is not easy to say. He stops and looks at my cigarette and says: "Haven't you given those up yet?"

"They're probably no worse than Sarotex," I say, "or what do *you* think?" And the next moment I repent my words because his face goes blank, its calmness gone, and he takes one step forward and then one back, he moves his mouth and is about to say something, and then he says nothing. I lower my eyes and look at the cigarette I hold between my fingers, stub it long and thoroughly on the saucer and look at the floor while I slowly get up from my chair. Then I look up again, and we stand staring at each other. His body grows heavier, his back bends, and his brow sinks, as if filled with the most terrible thoughts in the world and he alone had to carry them on his shoulders as the only man with a painful past, and I suddenly do not feel repentant any more. It was well said, I think, goddamnit, it was well said, and *that* he can read in my eyes, for he clenches his hands and red spots appear on his pale face, and then he comes quickly towards me and with full conviction hits me on the chest with a clenched fist so hard I have to take one step back.

"You stupid ass," he says, "you damned halfwit, you selfish little shit," he says, hitting me again and still harder now, and I stand with my back against the table and can go no further and have to make a decision pretty quickly. I hit him back. Right on the chin.

Maybe not that hard, but just hard enough. It feels good. He jumps back, and I hit him once more. In his stomach this time. I do not know what he had expected, but he did not expect this. He bends over with his hand round his chin, and I slip away from the table to the middle of the room with my hands clenched and raised in front of my chest before lunging out again like my father did in the photograph above the radio at home when the world was young and he was still younger; his crazy body naked to the belt with its shining shoulders and dancing feet and dancing curls and his left arm straight out in a punch like a battering ram. Or as in the picture cards I found in a bundle in a box in the attic; one card for each position with arrows for foot movements and arrows for the angle and direction of the arms, like a dancer's beginner's course, really, foxtrot, waltz and cha-cha-cha, but here on small cards with descriptions underneath in tiny writing: straight left, left hook, right hook, uppercut, and so on, there were at least ten of those cards in all, and I can see them clearly before me now, and once or twice some years ago I tried them out for myself, step by step, blow by blow, behind a closed door and felt like an idiot. Maybe that's what I *am* now, but I do not feel like it. I dance round my brother who straightens up with a confused look in his eyes. He coughs after the blow in the stomach and tries to catch my eye and twists round as I keep on dancing, and I hit out a few times into the air.

"Selfish. Am I selfish? What about you trying to get out of everything and leave me alone. What about David? You fucking prick," I shout, and he lets out a roar and throws himself at me, and neither right hook nor straight left or any other blow I know is of any use, for he lands on my chest and I go down with him, and we fall on his elegant floor and roll around. I go on hitting out while he wraps his arms round my chest so hard I can scarcely breathe. My side really hurts and I am close to howling. I twist as much as I can and roll us on until we meet one table leg and push the table along the floor right over to the bench where it stops and starts to crack, and then the leg breaks, and the table tips down over our heads. My brother lets go, air comes squealing into my lungs, and he screws himself into a sitting position holding on to the edge of the table and shouts: "Have you any fucking idea how much that table cost me?"

I sit up with a hand to my side and push myself out from under the table. Carefully I breathe as deep as I can, but it is not easy, for my heart is beating wildly, and with each lungful of breath I feel a stab to my side.

"How much did it cost?" I weakly ask.

He looks at me, and then at the table, he is breathing as hard as I am, and then he says: "Fuck the table," and gives it a kick, and it tilts up and stops on its edge, and the broken leg comes right off and falls to the floor with a sound like a bamboo bell in the forest, one early morning, in China or someplace. "I've never really liked it. It is too posh. It is just that I can't afford anything new right now. It is starting to look empty in here."

"I have the old kitchen table from Veitvet in the cellar," I say. "You can have that."

"The one with the stylish chairs from the forties?"

"Yes."

"God. That would have been great. I thought we had sold that."

"That was the idea. But I took it. I thought you had enough."

He looks round him at the walls of his house. "I probably had," he says, and rubs his chin, shakes his head and says: "Fuck me. Where did you learn that boxing stuff?"

"From the old picture of Dad that used to hang above the radio. I've got it in my bedroom. I always look at it before putting out the light."

"You're joking."

"Yes," I say.

"I don't remember that picture. Are you sure it hung above the radio?"

"Of course I am."

He shakes his head again and stays sitting on the floor brushing dust from his shirt front and smoothing his tousled hair back with his fingers. He does not look like he has seen the Light any more, but neither does he look like Jesus on the Cross just before crying: "My God, my God, why hast thou forsaken me?"

He says:

"Are we done with all this now?"

"Oh, yes."

"Good. I am too old for this sort of thing. But you always had a big mouth."

"Yes," I say, feeling oddly pleased. It is easier to breathe, I can take in air without trouble now, only the knuckles on my right hand feel sore.

"Look," he says, "I don't feel like going out any more. If we are going to drink we can do it here. I have a bottle I've kept."

"Under the bed."

"No, not exactly." He smiles slightly.

"That's fine by me," I say. "Can I smoke?"

"Of course you can."

He gets stiffly to his feet. His legs are trembling. He brushes dust from his trousers. Then he rubs his face.

"You just stay there," he says. And then he turns and walks out of the kitchen and downstairs to the basement room. His steps are not so light, but not so heavy either. I lie down on my back and stretch my body until it creaks and look up at the ceiling. I suck my knuckles. I could join a boxing club. They just might have a class for old boys. I could cut down on the smoking. Let's say, with five cigarettes a day. There's a lot of health to be gained right there. I sit up again and bump along on my behind and lean back against the cupboard smoking a cigarette and listening for my brother's steps. Here he comes.

He has a three-quarters-full bottle of Famous Grouse in his hand. He opens the cupboard above my head and takes out two kitchen glasses and gives me one. He sits down with a groan and leans his back against the fridge and unscrews the bottle. He fills my glass and then he fills his own.

"I'm selling out my share in the firm," he says. "It's a long time since I did my bit anyway. It's no fun any more. Besides, I'm broke."

"So what will you do?"

"I don't know. Actually, I like it like this; cleaned out, rock bottom."

"Welcome to the club," I say. He smiles, but his eyes are shining. He raises his glass.

"Rock bottom," he says.

I look down. I see my hand round the glass, the glass is full, but at least it is not gin. I raise my glass.

"Rock bottom," I say. I lean forward and let my glass touch his, and then we take the first mouthful, and I do not say anything about Mrs Grinde, or Naim Hajo for that matter. *That* would have been selfish.